The Colours
of
Orange

JACQUELANE COX

D.O.L.L.

WOMEN

book series

D.O.L.L.

Daughters of Love & Light
www.daughtersofloveandlight.com
Adelaide, South Australia
admin@daughtersofloveandlight.com

© Jacquelane Cox 2021

ISBN: 9780645252736

Cataloguing-in-Publications entry is available from the National Library of Australia
http:/catalogue.nla.gov.au

First edition published 2021

Dedication

for my family — always;

*and Dae, whose resilience
and adaptability inspires me;*

*and June
— a source of constant encouragement.*

'For I know the thoughts that I think toward you, says the Lord, thoughts of peace and not of evil, to give you a future and a hope.'

Jeremiah 29:11

Orange:

1. the colour of the sun's citrus glaze on a hot summer's day, of spring as the flowers wake; the colour of leaves falling in the autumn breeze … and the carrot on a snowman's nose.

2. Also, a regional city about two hundred and fifty kilometres west of Sydney, in Australia.

Prologue

March. Sydney.

Priscilla Bonifacio inhaled deeply. Desperate to contain her excitement, she took slow, controlled steps towards the beginning of her *happily ever after*. Michael's eyes were locked on her, and in that moment she understood what it meant to be overwhelmed by love.

She was grateful for the arm of her mentor's husband, who offered to walk her down the aisle. Her aunt and uncle, the last of her relations, couldn't – *didn't* – want to be here … But that was another story, and she wasn't going to let that ruin her wedding day. She would put that aside for now – for Michael, who clearly adored her. For his parents, who had already embraced her into their circle, and treated her as though she was their own daughter. And for the family and community she had been blessed to have met and been surrounded by since she arrived in Sydney. Yes, she may not have natural family in this foreign land, Australia, but she had enough people who loved her.

And as Stan passed her hand to Michael, the surge of electricity that coursed through her whole body sealed the beauty and truth of it all. She was his, and he was hers. How could she thank the God who had saved her and then opened her eyes to the wonderful human being she was to spend the rest of her life with? Michael had been her friend for over a year. But not until they both committed their life to the Lord did it dawn on them that they wanted to bring their two lives together.

God had done that, and He was the one who would be the centre of their married life.

She said her vows, promising her love, commitment and faithfulness – in sickness and health, 'til death; then the rings were given, the papers signed. And, of course, the kiss.

'Are you ready for this?' their minister asked after what seemed like a long ceremony.

'Been waiting for a while!' Michael grinned, his gaze on her clear with sweet intent.

He lifted the veil, and in the moment all the nerves, the excitement all frayed and faded. For that moment in time, it was just the two of them. Until, eventually, the clapping and cheering grew so loud they were brought back down to earth.

'You've rehearsed, haven't you?' the minister kidded, and they laughed.

They were announced husband and wife as the recessional music blared from the pipe organ. Her heart fluttered at the thought that she was now – officially – *Mrs Priscilla Robertson, wife of Dr Michael Robertson.*

She would be grateful for him. For this beautiful man that God had given her the privilege to love and be loved by. Grateful for the rest of her life.

Chapter 1

January.

Susan watched her daughter-in-law walk down the aisle to the altar for the second time in only twenty-two months. The first time had been a happy occasion for all of them. Michael Robertson, her son, had married his beautiful bride, Cilla, in a fairy-tale wedding, ready to start their life of bliss.

This time, in the same church, Susan's heart was torn and bleeding. She watched the twenty-four-year-old widow weep quietly over her son. Beside Michael's coffin, her own husband's coffin lay. Peter, the love of her life, was also taken from her. A horrible tragedy that shouldn't have happened.

Yet, the Lord had let it.

Peter and Michael weren't due back for another week from their holiday. And yet, here they were, being farewelled at a double funeral. A most heartbreaking circumstance. Two shiny coffins, father and son, side by side, was all that remained of their beloved.

Susan took a deep sigh and managed to complete her eulogy with only a few pauses. As she returned to her seat, the tears fell freely, and Cilla's arms enveloped her. Both of them trembled as they suppressed sobs of grief.

When it came time for Cilla's speech, she handed a folded paper to a friend and let her read it. Cilla visibly shook, kept her anguish silent as tears fell, listening only to the words she'd written. Listening to her sentiments but not her voice.

'It's okay.' Susan drew Cilla closer with one arm and kissed the top of her head. She waved the program back and forth to fan Cilla. 'It's okay to cry.'

The air conditioning circulated cool air, but it was a hot summer day in Castle Hill. The sporadic breath of wind was a sweet relief as they stepped out of the church and headed to the crematorium.

Dazed through the rest of the formalities, Susan found herself sitting beside Cilla back at the church's garden room. Sympathisers farewelled them. Their sentiments were the same, meant to comfort, but the words didn't penetrate at that moment. Beside her, Cilla was just as robotic, her face fixed with a polite smile, but her eyes empty.

'Oh, Susie.' A familiar voice from the past drew her to the present.

Susan lifted her head and focused her eyes. 'Helen? John?' Relatives from out of town. They would have travelled several hours just to be here. A roller coaster of emotions raced through her body, her mind's eye seeing flashes of bygone days, time forgotten.

Helen responded by hugging her, long and tight. 'I'm so sorry for your loss.'

And Susan felt she was sincere. When John hugged her, she broke down. John was Peter's second-cousin, although Peter had called him Uncle. John and Peter's father were cousins and very close, but Peter's father had died far too early. When Peter and Susan moved to Sydney, Peter and John continued to communicate via letters, and later via email.

As Susan wiped away her tears, she remembered Cilla and introduced her daughter-in-law. Cilla politely greeted Peter's relatives, but Susan could tell that her eyes were not seeing nor her ears hearing any of it. She hugged Cilla to her side to reassure the young woman.

Stepping aside, Helen introduced a man who looked a little older than what Michael would have been. 'This is our youngest, Andrew. Although, not so young anymore.' Mother and son shared an affectionate smile.

Susan's heart ripped some more. Had their own son grown up with him, Susan suspected they may have been friends. The same Robertson stature, hair and smile. She could see a little of Michael in him, and her whole being longed to embrace her own son again. She found herself drawing Andrew to her and embracing him.

Andrew expressed sincere condolences, then turned his gaze on Cilla. Susan introduced them, and once again Cilla was polite, but it was as if her soul had left her. Susan smiled up at

Andrew, her eyes pleading with him to appreciate the plight of the young woman widowed too soon. Andrew seemed to understand, and his own expression was full of compassion for the two of them.

'Thank you so much for coming all this way.' Susan's eyes began to moisten again. She resorted to hugging, her throat tight with emotion, then watched as Andrew ushered his parents away.

Beside her, Cilla maintained the same mild expression, a very polite and controlled smile on her face, as they continued to say goodbye to people. Susan worried, because deep inside she knew, Cilla's fragile heart was in a million pieces. And she wondered, would Cilla's fresh faith carry her through this test?

Chapter 2

February.

Cilla put her makeup on, getting ready to face another day without Michael, her husband of not even two years.

With great effort, she'd been gathering what remained of her life. And because of her faith, she wasn't entirely lost. But losing her only love, her confidant and best friend had slammed her heart into the wall. Her world had stopped. Then spun. While the initial process put her world in slow-motion – seeing him, identifying him, and allowing reality to sink in – the rest had happened in a blur; the funeral preparation, the legalities, the business end that had rendered the process so clinical. Cold. Impersonal.

When the fog had dissipated from her mind and the heaviness had lifted from her chest, she remembered Susan, her mother-in-law. Not only was she grieving the loss of her only son, she had also lost her husband of thirty-five years.

Cilla recalled how she and Susan had planned the men's road trip a year ahead. Both doctors, they didn't take many days off, committed to their regular patients and passionate about their work, their calling. Both couples were also committed to their local church, serving regularly in their congregation. Lately, the men hadn't had much of a chance to get away, so she and Susan had conspired and booked their accommodation along the road and spoken to their Practice Manager to ensure they weren't rostered at the beginning of the new year for three weeks. Three weeks of fun and relaxation cut tragically short by an accident, a drugged driver distracted by his phone on a quiet highway early one morning.

A morning like this, Cilla reflected. She should still be in bed, sleeping, but she couldn't sleep anymore. Awful dreams were sending her heart and mind racing.

So she had risen, showered, and put makeup on for the first time in what seemed like a lifetime.

And it *was* a lifetime. A lifetime since Michael was part of her morning, day and night. Cilla's life was different now. Without Michael, Cilla was living a new lifetime. Oh, but the pain was still excruciating, the wound still raw. A tear threatened to ruin her dark brown eyeliner and mascara. And she let it.

He was only twenty-nine. Why, Lord?

Cilla woke with a start. It was no longer early morning. It was way past breakfast time and Cilla's stomach was protesting, queasy and hungry even though her tastebuds were in no mood for food. Lately, everything tasted bland. She didn't want anything, and who could blame her. If she could, she would stay in bed, away from people, away from compassionate eyes that she knew loved her and felt for her. But for some time, particularly when it felt raw, she didn't want sympathy, kind words or even food. She wanted Michael back.

Their persistence in bringing her food, visiting her even just to sit and pat her head as she cried, or take her rubbish out ... had melted her heart.

Those kind souls from church, Michael's colleagues and patients, her friends ... they helped her break out of the darkness of her sorrow and self-pity while she grieved. Yes, she was still grieving, but she could breathe again. Most days.

She picked up her phone and clicked on the list of her most recent contacts. There was only one. She pressed on the photo and listened while the call connected.

'Hello?' The voice that answered her was gravelly. Cilla wasn't surprised that Susan had been crying.

'I'm going to pick you up in fifteen,' Cilla began with the same words she'd uttered for the last week.

'Can't do it ... yet.' Susan's voice broke on the last word.

Cilla sighed. Still the same response, but she wasn't going to give up. Susan needed to come up for air, she was wilting, spending days in her darkened home and not accepting visitors the last couple of days. She'd attended church only once more after the funeral. That day she had shown strength, even comforted those who cried on her shoulder, giving her own words of comfort, and assuring them she was fine. That should have been the biggest hint.

But Cilla had been in a wilderness of her own. In fact, she thought she'd be the one who would never recover; that Susan was going to be her pillar of strength from then on.

'We need to eat.' Cilla was firm.

Susan choked back a sob. 'I'm … I'm not hungry.' She cleared her throat.

Cilla picked up her bag and walked out of her bedroom. 'Have you got anything left in the fridge or freezer to re-heat?' They both had been well-provided for by the commiserating families.

'No. No more.'

That was a good sign. At least she was eating the meals given by well-meaning friends. She had already had some obvious weight loss.

'OK, I'll get something and bring it over instead. I'll be there in about half an hour.' Cilla continued to the garage. She was going whether Susan agreed or not.

'You don't have to.'

Cilla got in the car. 'I need to.' Cilla needed her mother-in-law to get back into living as much as she did. All they had were each other now. Susan didn't have family in Sydney as far as Cilla knew. No siblings, and her parents were both gone. When Cilla and Michael wed, there were some distant relatives introduced to her. But the day had been a blur of ecstasy, joy at marrying the man who made her feel loved to the core, her gift from God, the answer to her prayers. At the double funeral, she was numb and walked in a blur for days prior to and after the event. She didn't have a clue who was whom.

'Why don't you go see your friends?' Susan's suggestion was gentle, but Cilla knew it was a brush-off.

'I want to have brunch with you.' Cilla pressed the remote control and sunlight began to replace the dimness of the garage. Truth was, Cilla didn't want to hang out with her friends either. Not yet. She wanted to be able to give them a genuine smile when they next saw her. She didn't want to lie or see their pitying looks.

'Okay.' Susan always relented. As though she didn't have the strength to say no anymore, at least to Cilla.

Ending the call, Cilla took a deep, shaky breath and adjusted her mirrors. As she reversed out of the garage, the sun, in all its glory, shone on her, warming her whole body. It was as though God was caressing her hair and saying, 'I have not left you. I love you still. And I have a great plan for your future.'

She stopped as nausea hit her. The world spun a little. But she knew it would pass in a moment. With another controlled breath, she headed to the bakery Susan liked. She could share her news with her mother-in-law over croissants and Danish pastries and strong coffee.

Chapter 3

After successfully willing herself to sit up, Susan dangled her feet over her side of the bed. She didn't have time to touch Peter's pillows that still took pride of place beside her own. She had to shower, dress appropriately and be presentable before her daughter-in-law arrived.

This was probably the perfect time to tell Cilla her news. It couldn't be delayed any longer. She was quite determined. And with all the remaining legalities all going well under her solicitor's care, there was no reason to put off telling Cilla her plans.

After washing away tears in the shower and giving her face a bit of colour with makeup, she looked fresh enough and ready to tackle the world with strength and determination. She looked alive. She didn't feel it.

She prepared the coffeemaker and sat down. When she heard the engine of Cilla's car cut out in front, she pressed the remote control to open the garage. Cilla's shoes soon clicked on the tiles, and Susan pressed the button again.

'Hi!'

Upon hearing Cilla's voice, Susan put on a smile before turning around to greet her. They embraced, each absorbing strength from the other.

Poor girl. She's putting it on for me. Susan could feel the slight tremor from Cilla's body.

When Susan let go, she sensed Cilla's reluctance to end the hug. She felt Cilla's eyes on her as she walked to the coffeemaker and prepared two cappuccinos. She waited for Cilla to talk, but all she heard was the rustle of paper bags as Cilla pulled out whatever she'd bought for her. And Susan was determined to eat whatever Cilla bought, if only to please her. She needed to encourage the young woman, surely still grieving the terrible loss of her husband.

She caught herself before she shook her head. She looked up, gazed outside her window as she waited for the coffee to drip.

So young, she lamented. She and Michael had so much left to discover together and about each other. Before the mist in her eyes fell, she discreetly wiped them and chided herself. No, she needed to be strong – or, at least, be the appearance of strength – for Cilla, who had no one else. The poor girl only had an aunt and an uncle who lived in the Philippines. She had come to study at university and met Michael at a Bible Study that they'd both been invited to by a mutual acquaintance.

'We weren't interested in dating each other,' Cilla had related to her early in their relationship. Michael was intent on ensuring he followed in his father's footsteps and was in deep with his studies; Cilla was a Business student, keen on finishing her course and bridging her visa in order that she may get work and repay her aunt and uncle as soon she could earn a decent wage. But God had a different plan for the two of them. Cilla's earnest questions about Jesus triggered Michael's own questions about his faith. After a year of meeting with some of their Bible Study leaders, Cilla committed herself to Jesus and Michael's faith was revived. It was as though their new shared interest opened their eyes to each other and they began dating. Susan couldn't be happier for both her son and his girlfriend; but for Cilla, her aunt and uncle had considered her change of faith a betrayal.

Susan sighed as the memory of *that* tragedy flooded back. Cilla's relatives threatened to cut off their financial support, and when she didn't turn back, they saw it as willful disrespect and did cut her off. She had already finished most of her subjects and was working as many hours as her visa would allow. But without their full support, Cilla wouldn't be able to finish and she would have to go back home. Back where she would not exactly be welcomed with open arms. How anyone could turn their back on such a beautiful soul, Susan could not comprehend. She wanted to embrace her into her own fold back then but knew that it wasn't her place to suggest anything to Michael. However, God had plans.

Michael had spoken to Susan and Peter after some months, when the end of one semester approached.

'Mum, Dad, you know I am in love with Cilla,' he'd said, making Susan's own heart flutter. A romantic herself, she had a hunch about what was coming.

Before Michael could say any more, Susan asked him directly, 'Is she in love with *you*? Is she genuine?' Susan had no doubts, but she wanted to hear her son's thoughts. She was a picture of calm, but she could barely contain her excitement.

'From what I've learned of her over the last two years, she is nothing but an honest, trustworthy and loyal girl—'

'Except, of course, when she *betrayed* her aunt and uncle.' Susan was being facetious, but she regretted saying it immediately. 'I'm sorry. I should not have said that.'

Michael smiled kindly.

'And do you both love the Lord first?'

Michael had looked deeply into her eyes, the mirror image of her own blue ones. 'I can answer for myself, with all honesty, that I have found the one who fills the emptiness in my life – and that is not Cilla. I trust God and Him alone. I love Cilla, and I entrust her to Him.'

Susan smiled back at him, warmth filling her body and soul.

'Would you have any objections if I …' His voice faded, the question left unfinished.

'None.' Susan was elated to finally have said it, barely able to contain herself.

Michael had taken Cilla over to have dinner with them on several occasions and, over time, Susan and Peter had grown to love her as well. She was well-mannered, respectful, and indeed beautiful inside and out. 'Ask her soon. Don't let her leave the country or you may lose her.' Susan had smiled and winked.

Peter had simply hugged his son and slapped him on the back with deep affection. The red glow on his face and the mist in his eyes clearly indicated he was pleased. A man of few words who wore his heart on his sleeve.

While Michael went away to fulfill his rural requirements to achieve accreditation to becoming a GP, Peter and Susan offered to accommodate Cilla, who'd become like a daughter to them. God had worked out the rest.

Susan smiled at the memory, so bittersweet. And there were so many other memories here … the scent of dinners made together, private jokes, a son's entire lifetime. It hurt like … hell.

Sipping their cappuccinos and nibbling on their pastries in silence, Susan snuck a glance at Cilla. She cleared her throat. Now or never.

'I need to let you know—' Susan started at the same time Cilla announced, 'I have something to tell you.'

Cilla smiled in her sweet, shy way. 'You first.'

Susan shook her head. 'No, darl, you've got some news?' She picked up her cup and sipped, savouring more of the hot beverage.

'I want to hear from you first. You seem … excited about something.' She reached for Susan's hand. 'I miss your smiles.'

Had she smiled? Perhaps she had. Perhaps the thought of a change was giving her something to hope for.

'I'm thinking of moving back to Orange.' There it was. There was no reason to beat around the bush about the tree change she'd been tossing and turning about in the last couple of weeks.

Cilla paled. Her smile wavered then disappeared. 'O-Orange?' She made it sound like a foreign place.

Susan nodded.

'Orange? Is … is that a real place?'

Susan widened her smile and nodded, some new emotion filling her. 'It's where I come from.' She watched closely as Cilla's eyes began to enlarge … and mist. 'I was born there, grew up there, met Peter there.' She lifted a shoulder, then let it drop. 'Seems like the right time to return.' She was silent a time before she added in a much softer voice, 'Bring his ashes home.'

Cilla blinked. Susan could see the younger woman's facial expression change with the various emotions she must surely be wrestling with right then.

Finally, Cilla blurted, 'But, why?' Her voice was choked with shock and denial, and restrained with the ingrained respect that Cilla had always shown her. 'Your home is here.'

Susan looked away. 'This is not home anymore, Cilla.' She shook her head. 'I have nothing left here.' The emptiness threatened her again, and she fought it away. 'I can't bear the pain anymore. I have nothing … and no-one left.'

'Your friends. Your church.'

Susan shook her head, looked down at the table, and let a tear slide out of the corner of her eye. 'No. I have *no-one*. God has taken all that I have.' She bit her lip. She had allowed her emotions get the better of her. She wanted to apologise but she couldn't take her words back.

Cilla sounded as though she'd choked. When Susan dared to look at her, she was fighting for control. 'What about me, Mum?' Her chest heaved in and out with restrained emotion. 'You have me. Am I nothing to you? Will I not look after you? *You* are my family.'

Susan looked away again, out the window, to the blurry green outside, her thoughts far away. 'You have your own life. You can't waste it away, looking after me. I'll just be a burden to you.'

'You will not!' Cilla had thrown respect by the wayside.

Susan smiled impatiently. 'I have nothing left to give you!'

Cilla looked offended. 'What?'

Susan pulled herself together, shook her head and patted Cilla's hand with gentleness. 'You are young. You have so much life yet to live. You never know …' She hesitated. 'You will meet someone, and you should … or could remarry.' She watched her daughter-in-law's reaction closely. She didn't want to be crass. She knew that Cilla loved Michael deeply. But, the reality was Cilla was young and had so much love yet to give. She could have children … if she found another man to love. She deserved to have a family. And if she stayed, Cilla's fierce loyalty to her may hinder her from moving on.

Susan softened her tone some more. 'Besides, I want to retire somewhere pleasant and less hectic than here.'

Cilla's eyes misted again. 'You … don't want me with you.'

Susan snapped. 'Oh, don't be silly. I'm getting old and—'

'You're not even sixty!' Cilla wasn't the type to interrupt. Susan put it down to shock and more grief.

She continued, 'I need to think about the next chapter.' She turned her head as her eyes threatened to betray her affection for her daughter-in-law. 'I have been nothing but a wife since I married Peter, and a mother since Michael was born. My life revolved around them, and I doubt I'll find anything to take up my time now. Meanwhile, your life is here. And you've got plenty of it to live yet.'

'So do you!'

Susan swiped her hand in front of her face. 'I want to get old without all the pollution and the city's fast pace. I'm going back to where I came from. And so should you!' She glanced at Cilla. 'And I don't mean that in a racist way.' She smiled to soften the harshness of her words. 'You've got your church friends and old friends from university. Those are your roots here.'

Cilla was silent for a time before she spoke again. 'I didn't ... didn't realise.' She fumbled for words. 'I'm so sorry. I should have been more attentive to you. I should have been more supportive of you.'

Susan shook her head. 'No, no, no. This is not your fault.' A tear escaped her as she watched the younger woman cry for her. 'You've got your own suffering you're going through. But you're young. You've got a lot of things going for you. Whereas, me …' she paused, looked around her and swallowed the lump that had formed in her throat. 'Everything here reminds me of him. This home, our church, our friends … the women, the young ones. Everything and everyone.'

Cilla's head was shaking slightly from side to side, as though denying every word that Susan had just said. 'I'm coming with you,' she announced with determined finality, as though she had been processing this decision the whole time and had come to this obvious conclusion.

Susan blinked, caught by surprise. This was certainly not the response she'd anticipated. Objection and arguing, and tears of course, but not this. 'Are you kidding?' Cilla's expression told her otherwise. 'What would you do in Orange?'

Cilla smiled with confidence, brushing away tears. 'I'll find whatever work. I'll take whatever job there is. I'm not staying here without you.'

'No.' Susan shook her head, indignant for Cilla's sake. 'I'm leaving you, can't you see?' Her plans did not include dragging her daughter-in-law along to goodness-knew-what. 'I've got family there. You don't!'

'You've got family there?' Cilla now had a look of expectation.

It became apparent that Susan hadn't spoken much about her life before they moved to Sydney. And Michael had been born in Sydney, so he wouldn't have had much to tell about Orange. They'd all been consumed by the fast life that had them at a hustle-and-bustle pace when they first arrived in Bankstown, then eventually moved to Castle Hill, where Peter finally settled as a GP with a new Medical Centre. It was in Castle Hill they'd also planted themselves in a church and met many of their current friends.

Cilla wiped one last tear dangling on her chin. Susan's heart ached for her. Although she had no family connections in Australia, she had made many friends from church and university. She hadn't pursued a career after she married Michael, instead becoming his book-keeper and managing their finances while she volunteered much of her other time supporting the youth and children's ministers. What would she do in Orange?

Susan sighed. 'You won't survive the lifestyle – or lack of!' She eyed Cilla. Her daughter-in-law now had a grin on her face, determination beaming from her. Susan shook her head. But she couldn't deny the excitement beginning to bubble inside her. Could she and Cilla make a new start back in Orange? Would Cilla adapt to something so different from what she'd known?

She eyed her. 'Look … I know you're resilient, but …' She had seen the girl's perseverance. Cilla had moved to a totally different country, a very different culture, and had adapted well on her own. Then she had fitted right in with their family, their church community and she saw how well-loved and appreciated she was by all those who knew her.

Deep down, she had a feeling Cilla could adapt to more changes. Deep down, Susan felt it would all work out. She hoped her feelings would prove to be right.

As Cilla's eyes bore deep into hers, awaiting her words, she reached out to the heavens in surrender. 'I hope I don't regret what I'm about to agree to.'

Chapter 4

March. Orange.

Cilla's news had to wait. Susan already had much on her mind, and Cilla wasn't sure how her mother-in-law would see her pregnancy. If she was trying to leave the past behind, to forget the pain of losing Michael and her husband, then it may be more painful than not to hear of something that would so inextricably connect them to Michael. Besides, Cilla reasoned, she ought to wait for the traditional twelve weeks before telling Susan.

She determined to support Susan wholeheartedly with the move. It would be a distraction for both of them. And before long, she was on her way to Orange.

Cilla thoroughly enjoyed her drive through the gorgeous Blue Mountains and then the rolling hills from Lithgow to Bathurst. It felt so free, quite open in some places, and wild! A different sort of wild to the city. When she finally reached the outskirts of Orange, she breathed a sigh of contentment. This place was now going to be home. She didn't mind the thought of that. There was something nostalgic about the environment here.

It was early autumn and some trees were already hinting at their beautiful shades of reds, oranges and browns. She couldn't wait until the season was in its full glory.

She was at the lights near the shopping centre when the car began to smoke. Cilla looked around to see where it was coming from. The bonnet! And from under the car. And, looking in her rear-vision mirror, from behind. Her mind blanked. She couldn't think of what to do. Panic set in and she switched off the engine. The smoke began to clear. But she couldn't stay at the lights. She was almost there, according to the GPS, surely she could make it.

The light turned green. She switched the engine back on and pressed the accelerator, moving slowly on the road. Soon the smoke flowed out around her car again.

Taking deep breaths to keep her panic at bay, she pressed the hazard button and moved to the side, allowing the cars behind to pass.

But one car slowed right next to her and motioned for her to pull over a little farther up the road, where there was a shoulder. She did so, and he followed, parking right behind.

Oh, dear. Please don't be a murderer. She caught that morbid thought and reminded herself that her car was clearly in trouble. Anyone with eyes could see she needed help. And because this was the country, people were likely friendlier than city folk and helped each other out. At least, that's what she hoped. And besides, they weren't exactly in a remote area.

Still, she pressed the button that locked all her doors and didn't get out as a man in a dress shirt and jeans approached. Surely an axe murderer wouldn't be so well-attired. Murder would totally ruin his outfit ... and *he* looked rather expensive for a country road. She stopped herself again, this time from judging. At the very least, she could take off in her car if he proved to have bad intentions. She *hoped* rather than trusted her get-away vehicle, though.

She lowered her window as the man stooped to look at her. The first thing she noticed was the pair of eyes peering at her. Clear as day, she would recall later, and they looked kindly at her. He looked in his thirties, much older than her, but she noticed next that his smile appeared genuine. For some reason she felt immediately at ease, as though they'd met before.

God's angels must have been around her, sending her someone to help in the middle of who-knew-where-Susan-wanted-to-hide!

'Hi, are you right?' the man asked.

Words that had bottle-necked in her throat in the last couple of months decided to flow at this very moment, as she found herself gush out disjointed and unfinished sentences. 'I was – the car just started – the smoke was everywhere! I didn't know what to do. I'm not sure – my husband—'

Her breath caught and she stopped speaking, her eyes threatening to spill a dam of sorrow. And for a moment, the man's gaze held hers a little too long. Then he looked away and turned to the bonnet.

'She'll be right. Looks like you've run out of water.'

Water! She nodded, relieved it wasn't going to cause her more trouble than she thought.

'Pop the bonnet and I can have a look for you.' He motioned with his head toward the dash.

Cilla opened her door, madly looking for a button or knob to pull to open the bonnet. Frantic that she couldn't find it and the man was now also looking around near her legs, verbal diarrhea struck again. 'Where is it? I can't remember where it is. Different cars! They all put it in different places. I'm just so frazzled.'

She'd sold her car and kept Michael's, since it was bigger. Why hadn't she–? She clamped her mouth shut and decided to actually think.

'Ah, there it is!' She must get better acquainted with the car to save herself future embarrassment.

'There you go,' the man with the clear blue eyes and kind smile said, walking to the front and pulling up the hood.

Cilla stepped out of the car to appear helpful. She felt so foolish for having her situation get to this.

'My husband usually ...' She found herself again faltering at the mention of Michael.

The man seemed to understand and assured her. 'It's all good. I've been in the same situation, so when I saw your car smoking and your hazards on, I figured you needed some help.' His smile calmed her.

It must be the relief of getting some help in this alien environment that was causing her to swoon at her hero. He was much older than Michael—. Again, she stopped at the comparison, berating herself. She swallowed the lump of sadness that clogged her throat. She blinked repeatedly, willing the moisture in her eyes to evaporate.

The man began to walk back to his car. 'I always carry some water in my car, so at least I can help you with that.'

Cilla gathered her wits. *Get a grip!* 'Th-thank you!'

He came back and began to fill a container under the bonnet. 'See, that's your radiator,' he said as steam began to fizz out from the engine. 'It's just cooling it down. I won't fill it, as the car is very hot. When you get home – are you close to home?' He looked at her as though he doubted home was anywhere around here. He would have been right, but that was about to change.

She pointed in the approximate direction of *home*. According to her GPS, she had only a few turns to go … up the road. 'Yes, just up the road.' How long the road was could be another matter altogether, but she didn't want to elaborate. After all, she didn't know him.

'Well, you should get home all right,' he nodded, his smile infectious. 'But let her totally cool down before you put more water, otherwise you'll get all this steam again.' He looked straight at her. 'Like I said, this happened to me as well, so I know it's going to be fine. You've just ran out of water, that's all.'

I've just ran out of dignity, that's all. She made a note of checking the radiator regularly from now on. She no longer had a husband to rely on to get the car checked. At this thought, her eyes couldn't hold back the mist. 'Thank you,' she managed to choke out. 'I hope I didn't make you late for anything.' She motioned to his attire, hoping to shift the attention from her.

'Uh, no, it's fine. I'm on my way home, too. I just live up the road as well.' But he pointed in the opposite direction. 'I missed my turn just there, because I wanted to make sure you were okay.' He closed the bonnet.

Certainly must be an angel. 'Thank you,' she whispered and got in her car. She paused, gathering her thoughts, reminding herself of her destination. It had been a long drive from Sydney.

She became wary as the man stood by her window, waiting. 'I want to make sure it starts.' He motioned for her to start the engine.

Oh, of course! When her car started purring again without a hint of smoke, she looked back up at him. His eyes now looked a stark bluish-green, his smile warm. Why she was noting those things, she couldn't explain. But the impression he made would stay with her.

And she chided herself. She was a grieving widow after all. She missed her husband with the greatest ache in her heart and soul. She longed for his embrace. She yearned to see his smile, his eyes. To touch his hair and cheek, and hear his laughter … But that was all gone. He was gone.

As the stranger turned his car and drove away, Priscilla found herself caressing her still-discreet belly. Michael may be gone, but he'd left her with so many beautiful memories.

And the promise of his legacy.

Chapter 5

April.

There were several times Susan had questioned her reasoning for having allowed Cilla to join her in Orange. Like a month ago when she'd had to accept help from a total stranger because of her car! What if that man had other intentions? And now, after several weeks of watching her get up in the mornings and search for something to do and somewhere for them to go, she wondered if she'd been tricked by her own desire to be needed. She couldn't have just let Cilla stay in the city where she had connections, where she had the lifestyle that she was used to. Where perfectly able and promising young ladies ought to be!

What was she going to do here, except maybe waste away, looking after her poor old mother-in-law?

And yet, she was grateful – no, overwhelmed – at Cilla's commitment and loyalty to her. How she wished her son had lived to see what a wonderful woman he'd married. Perhaps that was it. Perhaps Cilla was lavishing on her the love she had for a husband who could no longer have it.

I must find her a husband.

Susan chided herself immediately. It had been merely months since her son's passing and she was thinking of his replacement for her daughter-in-law. Cilla would be grieving just as she was. But unlike Cilla, she was old and had had over three-and-a-half wonderful decades with her husband. Cilla didn't deserve to be widowed so young. *In time, Susan,* she resolved, *all in good time.*

As though the very idea gave her new purpose, she nodded and sipped her coffee as Cilla – who was shuffling still-unpacked boxes from one room to another, trying to clear the lounge room so that visitors had a place to sit, if they visited – continued to fuss around her. Cilla had left all her life in the city to ensure her own life was comfortable. And indeed, Cilla was a comfort. But Susan couldn't let Cilla's existence revolve around hers. She would make connections again here soon when she was ready, she was sure of it. But she had to ensure that the girl would also be well-connected, find her own circle of friends and make a life for herself here. Perhaps even find love again.

She drank the last drops of her coffee, got up and placed the empty cup in the sink, and helped Cilla with unboxing the last of the kitchen items. Not that they were going to be doing a lot of baking soon, but what else did they have to do but organise the pantry.

They worked in silence, absorbing the ambience of their new home. Susan had agreed to forgo her plans of living in one of the local retirement villages and lease a newish three-bedroom home near the Botanic Gardens instead. She must admit the place they both liked wasn't too bad at all. It was nothing like what either of them had in Castle Hill. But this place was cozy. They could make it a home.

She cleared her throat, the silence beginning to unease her. 'Well, what do you think, Cilla? Do you think we can survive in this *quaint* little house?' She smiled to lighten the mood.

Cilla beamed. 'It's … cozy.'

Susan smiled at that. Cozy indeed.

Cilla looked around. 'We'll make it home, don't you worry.' She stopped and looked at Susan with a tentative frown. 'But if you find yourself at any time uncomfortable, we'll find something else! Just let me know.'

Susan placed cups on a shelf before reaching to touch Cilla's arm. 'It's lovely, Cilla.' She smiled as she fought a tear trying to escape. Really, Cilla's fierce loyalty was going to break her down to a gooey puddle.

'And if you don't want to rent anymore, let's look at finding something to buy.' Her daughter-in-law continued to unpack and sort, sounding as though moving was the easiest thing in the world.

Susan's eyebrow raised a fraction before she smoothed it back to a neutral position. 'That seems like a long-term decision.' She turned away to put more cups on the shelf. 'You don't need to rush. Who knows …' she hesitated, 'you may find yourself yearning to go back to the city.'

There was no response as Cilla rustled with the papers covering Susan's crystal glassware.

'*If* you ever feel like you miss the city, that is.' The last thing Susan wanted was to make Cilla feel unwanted. But she also didn't want her staying out of obligation. 'I really appreciate you being here.' She turned to Cilla. 'You know that, don't you?'

Cilla met her gaze and smiled. 'Yes, we've talked about this, Mum.' She stood up and placed some wine glasses by the sink. 'If you want to move back to the city, then we can move back together. Where you want to be, I'm going to be. I don't want to leave you. And since you're the only family I have, you're stuck with me!' Her smile brightened. 'Now, I'm sure we've exhausted this particular conversation. Let's not talk about it again.' She walked over to Susan and gave her a tight hug.

Susan turned away as soon as they let each other go. She discreetly wiped away a tear and started washing some dishes in the sink. Sniffing, she smiled at her own plans brewing. She'd find somebody for dear, sweet Cilla. And the sooner she got in touch with her old acquaintances and relatives, the sooner she can get the ball rolling.

Sighing, she thought about those she hadn't kept in touch with over the last three decades. Her cousins had welcomed her with open arms, but she and Peter had old church friends that she hadn't written or spoken with in ages. Though many of them were probably on Facebook or some such, she wasn't much for using social media; she hated the impersonality of it. Would those old friends welcome her too? Were they even still around?

'Shall we check out a few churches over the next couple of weeks?' Cilla's cheery voice broke into her musing.

The saucer almost slipped out of Susan's hands. It was soapy, she reasoned.

'Or have you got one already in mind?' Cilla continued with enthusiasm, unaware of her reservations.

Susan hadn't thought much about attending church. Her heart still ached. And she felt disconnected. So disconnected from the loving God she'd known and worshipped since she could remember. The death of Peter and Michael earlier in the year had not only ripped her heart out, it had smashed it to a pulp. Deep in the anguished vaults of her being, she knew a Truth. The truth that there was still the same loving God somewhere out there. But where was He in these circumstances? She'd felt cold, abandoned. Had the Lord turned against her? Perhaps not. But it felt like that.

'Any preference?' Cilla would be aware that she was hurting, but Susan hadn't let on to her that she didn't feel so keen about attending church for a while.

Susan wiped her hands and spoke slowly. 'Why don't you go and check out a few for me?' She kept her eyes averted. 'I think I just need some time to settle in. When you find one that you like, I'll come.' She headed to her bedroom. 'I'm just going to unpack a few more things in my room. Do you mind?'

'Are you okay?' There was concern in Cilla's voice.

Susan waved her hand, nonchalant. 'I just remembered something I need to dig out before

I forget about it.' And she hightailed it to her bedroom, just before the tears came pouring out.

Chapter 6

The first doctor she'd visited in Orange told Cilla her baby was a little smaller than the average but that there was nothing to worry about. She was healthy, the baby seemed healthy, and chances are the baby was going to be small because neither she nor the baby's father were very tall. She'd allowed herself to get teary upon discussing Michael. But the doctor understood and didn't press her with too many questions about him.

'Keep eating healthy and keep up your iron,' Dr Lee advised as Cilla left her office.

As Cilla drove around Orange, she familiarised herself with the town. 'You'll have to look after yourself now,' she mumbled. She had herself, a mother-in-law and a baby to look after, she corrected her thoughts.

The same cares and worries stirred in her mind. Would they be okay – two women and a baby? Of course, they would! Women had the instincts to care for babies and others since time began. They had a roof over their heads, and clothes on their backs. And each other!

Would their finances hold out? With the rent and groceries? Could they afford to buy a home eventually? A rental home wasn't secure. A landlord could decide to sell. Then they'd have to find somewhere else quickly. It wouldn't be good to keep moving with a baby, would it? She wondered if Susan had enough Super or pension or inheritance from Peter. But was that any of her business? Would it be rude to ask?

'Oh, Michael.' She found herself turning into the parking lot of the Botanic Gardens, only a few minutes from home. She sat in the car, taking deep breaths.

Michael had bought them a house and she'd had to sell. She would have moved into a unit and worked to support herself back in Sydney, being frugal with what little money

Michael's will had left for her. It was a challenge to find something she could afford, and it was likely she may have needed some assistance from the government to get by. When Susan made her decision to move, she'd at first panicked, wondering what she could do in the country town. But she had no second thoughts about staying in close contact with Susan. She knew, at such a difficult time, they needed each other.

Gathering her wits, she mumbled a prayer. 'God, you called me for a reason. I thank you for the privilege of knowing you. For knowing of your great love for me. I could not have gone through all this without you.' A hot tear dropped on her steering wheel. 'You called Dad and Michael *home* early for a reason. I don't know why. I don't know your reasons. It hurts so much. We feel lost without them. I could ask why you allowed all this, but there's probably no point at the moment. I need you right now. I need your peace and your comfort. God, I need your assurance that we'll be okay.' She allowed a fresh dam of tears to break, then sighed as the waterworks subsided.

Finally, taking her phone from her bag, she made a list.

Priorities:
Find a job
Pay off aunt and uncle
Save money

Baby:
Take iron supplements
Journal my pregnancy
Save money

Susan's cousins – Frances, Mary and Connie – adored Cilla. They thought she was 'a breath of fresh air', 'the bees' knees' and 'exactly what Susie needed.'

'Although, you've got to watch her,' Frances cautioned, knitting a loop in the cardigan she was making for a granddaughter.

Susan gave her an eye. 'Meaning?'

Frances waved a dismissive hand. 'I don't mean in a suspicious way. I mean, watch her mood and so on. She seems all held together. But who knows what's truly going on inside her head. She's just lost a husband. So young. She could get depressed and all that.'

Mary nodded and tutted. Then she shook her head. 'Yes, there's so much mental health issues these days. It's this generation. They've got too much on their minds.'

'I blame technology and all that.' Connie crocheted, her throw looking almost finished. 'Does she keep in touch with her friends in Sydney?'

Susan sat back on her recliner and sighed. 'I don't know, really. I haven't asked.' She looked at each of them. 'Should I ask?'

They nodded. 'It wouldn't hurt,' answered Connie.

'I just didn't want to intrude on her privacy.' Susan sipped tea from her cup. 'Mind you, she has been out and about. Exploring the town, she says, and getting familiar with everything so she knows where to go. She's so independent, which is a great thing for her. Imagine moving from one country to another, embracing a culture …'

'Embracing the Robertsons!' Frances grinned.

Susan smiled sadly. *Yes, the Robertsons.* She would have to get in contact with Peter's remaining relatives, see how they were going. She had been comforted by their presence at the funeral, grateful they had made the time and the journey to sympathise with them. *Uncle* John had been a favourite of Peter.

Wistful, she sat quietly and allowed her cousins to continue chattering, their voices blurring as she fought to maintain control of her emotions. It didn't matter that it had been three months since. The tears came sporadically now, but always when she least expected.

God, why did you let this happen? We devoted our lives to you. We gave everything. I thought we would live long lives, grow old – older than our late fifties – together, serving you, serving our community.

Discreetly, sipping her tea as a decoy, she wiped a tear under her eye.

I have nothing now. I have no-one. No-one to love, and no-one to love me.

Chapter 7

May.

Cilla parked the car at the corner of Summer and Clinton Streets, beside Cook Park. The environment of Orange beckoned to her to stop and marvel at the colours around, to breathe in the scent of a fresh autumn day, but she had work to do. Or rather, work to find.

Buttoning her trusty charcoal-coloured coat and wrapping her scarf about her shoulders, she set off on Summer Street where her map app showed her several dots that indicated cafes and restaurants. Armed with several copies of her resume in a plastic envelope, she mustered up the courage and entered the first eatery she passed.

The lady behind the counter at the cafe was all smiles when she walked in. But then eyed her when she told her she was looking for a job.

'Sorry, we have no opening.' She gave back the resume to Cilla.

'Would you mind giving it to your manager?' Cilla asked, especially sweetly.

She received a forced smile.

'Sure.' Her resume found itself on top of a pile of magazines by the register.

Cilla walked on, bracing for each rejection but not losing hope. There were a few places that had ads stuck to their doors and windows, indicating they needed casuals. There, Cilla walked out with a smile, her resume received readily.

It was half past eleven when she next looked at the time, after having been rejected outright or advised to send her resume via email for the umpteenth time. Not exactly lunch time yet, but she was hungry, her emotions ravaged, and the sweet and savoury smells she'd been walking in and out of had been tempting her taste buds.

She stopped in front of an establishment that looked a bit fancier than a coffee shop, but she admitted she had worked hard all morning and she deserved decent fuel. She also reasoned she had a long walk back to her car.

Warmth enveloped her as she entered the premises. Not just the comfortable temperature, but more so the cozy ambience and the tantalising aroma of comfort food. Her eyes travelled straight to the board with the day's special, her resume and job-hunting all but forgotten. Before she could read the board, however, someone came from the kitchen to welcome her.

Her jaw dropped, recognising his eyes, clear as day, and his kind smile. He, too, must have remembered her because he grinned wider and called out to her with familiarity.

'Hey, it's you!'

She gathered what was left of her rapidly leaking dignity and shook away the memory of her radiator running out of water. She managed to squeeze out a faltering, 'Hi,' making a mental note to schedule that next radiator check!

'Early lunch?' The warmth of his smile reached his eyes.

Cilla managed a nod and blurted out the first item that she saw on the board. 'The pumpkin and sweet potato soup, p-please.' Her stomach grumbled in agreement.

The man – whose name she hadn't even inquired about – motioned to a chair. 'Slow cooked pumpkin and sweet potato soup. Great choice. Mum's special recipe!' He pulled out a chair for her. 'Have a seat. Would you like a drink?'

'Uh…' Cilla hadn't had a chance to think of much else.

'Why don't I give you a chance to think about it. I'll get you some water in the meantime.' He was in the kitchen before Cilla could respond.

Her resume now sat on the white linen tablecloth, beside a wine glass and perfectly laid-out utensils. What joint had she entered? No, this was far from a joint. This place was elegant, classy and comforting all at once. And who was this Good Samaritan who'd rescued her on the road in the middle of nowhere, now suddenly appearing everywhere? Perhaps it was a sign that she should apply here. She touched the resume and looked around.

There were only three other patrons. Maybe they wouldn't need help, after all.

She could hear noise from the kitchen. Not unpleasant like an episode from some reality kitchen-nightmare show. More a buzz of activity. And wait, did he say Mum? He was working for his Mum? Surely he wasn't a student doing part time gigs for extra money. He looked all business-y when she first met him.

She told herself to mind her own business.

Sighing, she leaned back and allowed herself to contemplate, for the first time, how she and Susan could survive here.

'Water.'

She jumped at the sound of the man's voice.

'Sorry,' he chuckled. 'Didn't mean to scare you. Have you thought about what you'd like to drink … other than water?'

She shook her head. 'Water is fine,' she croaked, surprised how dry her throat was.

She sensed him hesitate before asking, 'How's your car?'

At this, she smiled. 'Great! And thank you again for helping me!'

'Pleasure.' He turned to go. 'Your order is on its way.'

'Thank you.' She sipped the water and returned to contemplating life away from the city. So far it seemed slow. She needed to do something. Craved to be active. If she didn't find a job soon, she would surely lose her mind. Hobbies and crafty things were good for a while, but those were for her down-time. What she needed was interaction … busyness. Anything to distract her.

There was also the business of finalising the debt she owed her aunt and uncle. Despite them disowning her, they hadn't complained about the money she had been sending them to pay back the tuition fees they'd initially invested. There was little left to pay, and even a casual job would finish that off in no time. Then she could just concentrate on working for the sake of working.

By the time she finished her lunch, the place was alive. Her Good Samaritan was assisted by two other people. Cilla saw that they could use her help. And she was willing to wait, wash dishes, do their shopping. Whatever.

She checked the time. If she ordered dessert, she could stay longer and perhaps speak to someone about a job. She discreetly rubbed her belly and prepared for a sweet treat.

Chapter 8

'How was it?' the friendly man asked Cilla after she'd relished the home-style apple pie with ice cream on the side.

'Lovely.' She wiped her mouth on the napkin and stood up. She followed him to the cash register to pay. *Now or never.*

Cilla cleared her throat. 'Um ...' she fidgeted inside her bag, looking for her wallet and some courage.

'Would you like anything else?' The man's easy smile held its usual warmth. 'Something for the road?'

Cilla chuckled and swallowed her nerves. 'Actually, I was ... uhm ...' She looked at him again as the thought hit her. 'Are you the manager here?' Why was she nervous? She'd walked in and out of several shops and cafes for the last few hours, courage buoying her from door to door. She could do this. 'I was hoping to leave my resume.'

'No, I'm not – but I can get *my* manager for you.'

Cilla waved her hand. 'Only if they're not busy. Otherwise I can just leave my resume.'

'Hang on a moment.' And he was gone before she could say any more.

She blew a strand of hair from her face and turned to look around her some more. She really did like the paintings hanging on the walls. It gave the coziness a bit of a modern edge.

'Hi, there, you're looking for some work?'

Cilla turned back and was greeted by another warm smile. A woman this time. She wondered if this was his Mum. But she didn't look that much older than him. 'Oh, hi. Yes! My name's Priscilla.'

'I'm Judy.' The woman shook her hand. 'Do you want to have a chat?'

Cilla was surprised at the spontaneity. 'S-sure.'

Judy led her to the quietest corner of the café, by the window. It wasn't long before the same waiter came and brought Judy a cup of coffee.

'Thanks, Drew,' she said, and Cilla took a mental note of his name. 'Any drink for you, Priscilla?'

Cilla shook her head. 'No, I'm fine, thanks. But please call me Cilla. Cilla for short.'

Drew – now she knew his name – left them.

As Judy quickly scanned through her one-page document, Cilla's heart beat a steady rhythm. She had been hopeful but, though welcome, an interview on the spot was unexpected. She should have dressed up a bit, instead of just black jeans and a plain black shirt. Today's errand was to leave her resume and then wait for phone calls over the week, not necessarily score an interview.

She cleared her throat. *Keep calm.*

'Robertson.' Judy said her last name with a questioning look. 'Are you in any way related to the Robertson family here in Orange?'

Cilla's eyebrows furrowed. 'Um …' Was this a trick question? Was she supposed to know the Robertson family of Orange? 'Um … I'm not sure.' She had nothing to tell but the truth. 'I – we, my mother-in-law and I, moved here a couple of weeks ago. She and her husband came from here before they moved to Sydney. Perhaps *they* have a connection.'

Judy nodded. 'Perhaps. Where in Sydney are you from? I moved here three years ago from Eastwood.'

Cilla grinned. This, she could easily answer. 'We're from Castle Hill.' She hesitated before saying more. Should she tell her why they'd moved? Perhaps she didn't need to elaborate too soon.

'And what brings you to Orange, then?'

Okay, so she *did* need to elaborate. 'Uhm …' Cilla fought hard to keep tears at bay. 'My husband—' Cilla's voice squeaked out as she said the words. She cleared her throat and continued.

'My husband and my father-in-law recently passed away—'

'Oh, I'm sorry.' Judy reached for her hand, then pulled back.

'No, it's okay.' Cilla cleared a tickle in her throat. 'My mother-in-law wanted to settle down here. So, I came with her. I wanted to be near her and support her... You know.' She gulped, wondering if she'd shared too much.

Judy nodded, her eyes sympathetic. 'I'm sorry,' she said again and turned to the resume. 'Says here you've done a lot of volunteer work. But have you done any waiting or other customer service?'

Cilla anticipated this question. 'While I haven't had much experience in that area, I've been involved a lot at my church with youth groups and children's ministries. I've helped leaders in organizing events, catering and interacting with different types of people. I've also done book-keeping and other administrative duties for my husband as well as church. And,' while she didn't want to seem desperate, she knew she had to add, 'I am ready to learn new things and adapt quickly.' Cilla held back a sigh. She sounded so trite! *Just like in an interview.*

Judy smiled at her. 'I can see you're brave and willing to do that. I mean… you moved all the way here!'

Cilla's heart pumped with hope.

Judy continued. 'I don't want to assume too much, but it sounds like you moved to Australia from somewhere else as well. That would have been a big transition, too!'

She let out a breath. Another topic she was comfortable with. After Cilla explained her background, they discussed other details she'd written on her resume. Judy's demeanour made Cilla relax. Still, she didn't want to get her hopes up too high. While she was very much willing to learn and throw herself in the deep end, a good interview didn't mean she would get the job. And she worried that her lack of work experience was a huge factor. Cilla knew she would be more than capable of doing whatever job was thrown at her because she was determined to work. But *if* they did need help, would Judy be willing to take a chance on her?

Chapter 9

Susan lay in her bed, eyes teary. She'd been reading the Psalms, revisiting God's promises. Her spirit was desperate for renewal like a drought-stricken land, cracked and waiting for even the lightest of showers.

She got up. Outside her window, the colours of Orange were only just beginning to fade from its palette of reds and browns and various shades of greens. While her eyes saw the spark of autumn, her heart could only envision a frozen landscape, a long, colourless winter ahead with no summer in sight.

'God,' she cried out, 'where are you in this?' She sobbed, the ache surfacing.

But there was no time to wait for His answer. Susan heard the front door open and shut. Cillla was back from her errand, and Susan needed to fix her blotchy face before she left her room. She supposed she could stay inside and pretend to be napping, but that wouldn't do. Cilla needed company after a day of job-hunting.

While she readied in front of her vanity table, she heard the younger woman busy herself outside. Cups clinking, stirring, and rustling of biscuit packets. Presently, she stepped out of her bedroom and was greeted by a beaming Cilla. *Ah, some good news, then.* She mustered up a smile in return.

'You've got something to tell me!'

Cilla's excitement was undeniable. 'Soooo much!'

Susan allowed herself to absorb Cilla's enthusiasm, and resolved to forget her sorrows long enough to celebrate with Cilla. Allowing Cilla to fuss over her, she soon had a steaming cup of strong, aromatic coffee, just what she needed. The excitement was palpable.

Cilla finally sat in front of her with a huge sigh, beaming and showing off her beautiful and exotic features for the first time in quite some time. Though they'd been grieving only a little over four months, it seemed a long time since she'd seen the young woman grin. Like a lifetime.

Well? she wanted to prompt. But she arched an eyebrow instead, a smile playing on her lips, too.

Cilla looked about to burst. 'I spent the morning walking door to door. Left my resume at different cafes and real estate offices…'

She had to give the girl credit. With no more professional experience other than what she'd done for her husband and all the volunteer work for different church ministries, Cilla was confident and courageous. Susan's heart swelled.

'I was getting a bit disappointed after the twelfth place I walked into. But I suppose, not many people expect walk-in applicants these days.' She shrugged. 'Oh, well. I needed a walk, anyway. And it's so beautiful right now. With all the leaves just hanging on. And the weather – just gorgeous! There *was* a bit of a chill, but the sun was beautiful.'

Susan grinned with nostalgia. She did love Orange and the different seasons here. She was glad Cilla seemed to be appreciating that, too. She liked autumn best, with the colourful foliage, and the leaves just waiting for that soft brush of wind to finally coax them off the trees. A couple of weeks and it would all be different.

'I didn't realise the time, but when I entered this café, it smelt *so* delicious, I suddenly remembered my stomach!' Cilla laughed. Again, the laughter was a welcome and comforting sound. 'I forgot all about looking for a job and got distracted by the menu!' Cilla went on with eagerness. 'Then – you wouldn't believe it!' Her eyes shone.

Susan mirrored her excitement.

'That same guy who helped me when my car was smoking? He works there!'

Susan chuckled. 'What a coincidence!' She finished her coffee and clasped her hands in front of her as she waited for Cilla's story to unfold.

'Anyway, I ended up eating. Food was awesome. The guy said the food there was his mum's recipes.'

Susan perked up some more. 'Really? What's the name of the café?'

Cilla stopped short. 'Oh!' She looked away, as though the answer was in the air. 'Um … I can't remember!' She laughed ruefully, looking perplexed. 'I can't believe I actually don't remember!'

Susan waved her arm. 'Never mind. Go on.'

'After I stuffed myself and remembered my resume, I got to speak to the manager. Can you believe it! We had a chat, and I think I convinced her that I'd do pretty much anything. I told her about us – not too much,' she added quickly, eying Susan with caution, 'just why we're here, since we came all the way from Sydney. Turns out, she's also from Sydney. She moved with her daughter, who got a job as a teacher at one of the local schools.' She took a breath and went on. 'So, here's the thing.'

Susan waited calmly, her clasped hands now under her chin as she watched her daughter-in-law's animation with pleasure. She had never seen her so full of life before, at least not lately.

She noticed Cilla hesitate. 'Would you be okay if I worked early mornings? I'll be finished by mid-afternoon and no working nights!'

Waitressing? Susan assumed. Cilla was a hard worker, there was no question, and she had no doubt the young woman could achieve whatever she put her mind to. But with her attitude and aptitude, Susan thought Cilla would have been looking for more of an office job. Something to do with what she studied at university. What was the likelihood of that at a café?

'Judy needs some help waiting tables. But I mentioned that I did Michael's book-keeping, so I may be able to assist her with the accounts stuff in the back.'

Susan nodded. She wanted to be as glad for Cilla, but she couldn't help the disappointment that crept in. Cilla was young, she could continue her studies if she really wanted. And the men hadn't left them destitute; she and Peter had saved enough over their life together. She had to make do until all the legalities were completed, but they would manage. In fact, they were financially safe and didn't need to work for some time, if at all. She wondered if Cilla knew that.

'Are … are you happy?' she asked in a guarded but – she hoped – an encouraging tone.

Perhaps Cilla would be happy with a more casual job simply to fill in time. She would observe how the girl went.

Cilla nodded. 'Oh, yes! I mean … I know I haven't done anything like waitressing before, but I love talking to people! Oh – guess what!'

'Yes?' Susan arched her eyebrows again. *More news?*

'Judy goes to a local church, and she invited us!' Cilla paused. 'I mean … *if* you would like to come. I'm happy to check it out first and tell you about it.' Her eyes were beseeching.

Could she say no? Could she snuff out the flame burning before her eyes? *Oh, God, am I ready?*

She felt Cilla's hands cover hers on the table. 'It's okay if you don't want to come. Maybe next time. I'll check it out. See what it's like.'

Susan smiled at their hands. 'No …' A myriad of excuses ran through her mind and was gone in an instant. She had to go. Whether she felt like *doing church* or not, she knew deep down God hadn't changed. Even though her heart felt like its blanket of security had been ripped off her, it still knew she was loved. She must go because her soul needed it, even if she didn't want to hear words so familiar to her she could still recite them. And she would go because Cilla needed her mother-in-law to walk with her during their time of grief. She would not abandon her, as Cilla's relatives had abandoned her. She would be the family that Cilla needed. They would be each other's anchor as they mourned their beloved men.

'I'll come.' Her words sounded more convincing than she felt.

The hands wrapped around hers tightened and she looked up into misty, dark brown eyes. A tear escaped and slid down Cilla's cheek.

'I have something else to tell you,' she said softly.

The look on Cilla's suddenly shy face was as illuminating as a million stars on a clear night sky. Susan's instincts kicked into gear and her heart leapt.

Chapter 10

Cilla's belly fluttered with three million butterflies. *Indigestion,* she convinced herself. She shouldn't have eaten dessert. And should completely cut out caffeine. Or perhaps, if she was honest, she was just nervous.

She felt the hands she was holding now squeeze hers. 'Tell me.'

Susan's face looked eager. Did she know? Could she tell? Cilla had put it off for so long, the timing never right. Susan had been so resolute about moving to Orange, desperate to leave Sydney and the past behind, to start afresh, that Cilla had kept delaying. Instead, she had focused on the tree change as well. So single-minded about convincing Susan that they should both embrace a new life *together* and psyching herself up as well for a move that seemed even bigger than when she came to Australia as a student. Moving to Orange – a place she hadn't even heard – was never on her radar. She may as well have moved to Iceland! No family connections or friends or plans. Or even a memorable past. But how could she part with her beloved mother-in-law, to leave Susan to fend for herself? How could she live without the only family she had left? They may not be blood, but marrying Michael only forged their connection stronger. And, of course, how could she bear to think of not allowing Susan to form an intimate relationship with her grandchild?

Before she could say any more, her tears poured out. She inhaled sharply and placed her hands on her barely-there belly. 'We're having a baby.' Deep joy and sorrow mingled, her tumbling emotions crashing into each other like stormy waves against the beach. While tears of elation flowed freely, a fist of grief squeezed her heart tight.

Susan stood and came to her. She welcomed the embrace, the warm hand rubbing her back, and took in the soothing and assuring words cooed over her. Cilla felt Susan shaking, felt tears falling on her own head as the woman who was now closer than any mother had ever been stood over her.

They remained speechless and allowed only their tears to speak what they couldn't. The happiness such news brought was also a reminder that they were still hurting.

When they let go, and Susan returned to her seat, Cilla chuckled. 'Michael didn't leave us empty-handed at all, hm?' She wiped her eyes and nose on a tissue. Sniffing and highly suspicious of her smeared make-up and reddened nose, she excused herself to wash in the bathroom.

When she returned, Susan looked ready to ask questions and hear more. 'How far along are you? Have you seen a doctor? Have you got a gyno?'

Cilla nodded. 'Five months. I knew when I started gagging for no reason. I checked with Claire straight away.' Dr Claire Foy was one of

Peter's business partners and close friend. It had been bittersweet for her, too. And even sadder when she confided that they were moving to Orange. But Cilla had promised her that she would bring the little one to visit once he or she was born.

'Have you got a doctor here?' Susan asked.

Cilla could see that the older woman's cogs were working.

'I think one of Peter's colleagues from way back is still here. Her name's Anne. I know she became a gyno. You should see her.' Susan paused. 'I mean, if you want to see a gyno. I'm sure the public hospital and the midwives here are great, too.'

Cilla assured her that Michael had arranged for the top health cover for them. If only Michael were there beside her now, sharing this news. She pushed away the wistful thought and looked at her mother-in-law.

Susan's gaze upon her was guarded.

Cilla furrowed her eyebrows. 'You seem concerned.'

Susan quickly put on a smile. 'Am I that transparent?' She raised her eyebrows. 'Yes, I'm just a little concerned,' she admitted. 'Will you be fine with waitressing? It's not that I don't think you're capable. You'd do well in anything. But…with being pregnant …' She hesitated. 'You know that you don't need to work, don't you? We can access some money now if we need it.'

Cilla gave her mother-in-law a reassuring smile. 'I know. The money is not really why I want to work. Partly, yes – because I want to feel like I'm doing something for myself financially. But I want to feel useful.'

'You've already been so useful to me!' Susan assured her. 'And if it's just something to do, maybe you can find a less strenuous job, a desk job. Charities like to have volunteers.'

'I need to do something different,' she insisted. 'I've got so many years of my working life to live, and I haven't had much experience other than working for Michael and helping out at church. I thought maybe I needed to find out what other things are out there. And…' Cilla hesitated about something she hadn't openly discussed with Susan before, but knew the truth would set her free. 'I know you think that my aunt and uncle are not very nice.' She saw Susan's eyes cloud over for an instant. 'But if not for them, I never would have been able to come to Sydney to study. I may never have met the Lord … or met your son and your family. I want to repay them for that debt.'

Susan sighed and looked away briefly. 'What about maybe going back to finishing your degree, then?' Susan suggested. 'Or trying a totally different course. I could help you. Forget about trying to earn money. Cilla, they disowned you.'

'No.' Cilla's eyes blazed with determination. 'I still owe them.'

Susan shook her head. 'I can help you. You don't need to work. Would you promise me you'll think about something long term … while you settle into life here?'

Cilla inclined her head. 'I did think about doing a different course. But I'm not sure right now.' She looked out the window. 'While I try to figure out what I want to do, I thought maybe I can do something casual and not too stressful.'

'But now that you're pregnant …' Susan eyed her, clearly weary. 'You didn't tell them, did you?'

'Oh, no.' Cilla shook her head. 'I figured they didn't need to know. Not yet. And I feel strong. Really, I do,' she insisted.

'Perhaps, you could postpone working until after the baby is born.'

'I'll be fine, Mum.' She gave Susan a smile, pleading with her eyes. 'I'm feeling strong, and I've always been healthy. Other than feeling a bit of nausea very early on, I haven't had any other issues. I'll make sure I stay safe and I won't do anything silly.'

Susan gave a reluctant smile. 'I just want what's best for you … And now, the baby, too.'

Cilla nodded in understanding. She got up and hugged Susan. Then, as she began to clear the snacks and coffee cups away, she remembered. 'Oh! The name of the café is *Helena's*. And it's owned by a family with our last name. Robertson!'

Susan's eyebrows shot up. '*Helena?*' Would there be an end to all of Cilla's surprises? 'We're related to a *Helen* Robertson!'

Chapter 11

June.

Nervous, excited and confident all at once, Cilla walked in silence beside her mother-in-law from their car towards the entrance of the church building. Sydney had many historic buildings like this one, splattered between more contemporary high-rises and structures. But in Orange, historic-looking was everywhere.

Judy greeted her at the door. 'Well, hello, friends!' Her embrace was so warm it thawed Cilla's freezing body to the core. 'This is my daughter, Cassia.'

Cilla returned Cassia's wave. 'How are you?' She figured the teacher wasn't much younger than herself and wondered if they could possibly forge a friendship.

'This must be your mother-in-law!' Judy extended her hand to shake Susan's.

'Yes, I'm Susan.' Her smile was sincere, but Cilla knew it was cautious.

Judy gestured for them to follow her in.

Inside were high ceilings over a spacious and modern auditorium, yet the mood was welcoming and friendly. There weren't pews as she'd briefly imagined but soft seats designed for comfort. The walls were white, crisp and clean. The stage displayed a few instruments. Although much smaller than the congregation that she and Susan had left behind, it didn't feel *dated* as she'd expected. She held back gushing her disbelief. Instead, she and Susan exchanged lifted brows and smiles.

Judy stopped and ushered them into a half-empty row of seats. Susan went first, and Cilla followed. Judy sat down next to Cilla and explained the usual order of service. Cassia sat by the aisle.

Soon, four people got up on stage and picked up their instruments.

Judy stood. 'Oh, by the way.' She pointed across the aisle and a little to the front. 'Over there are the Robertsons. Remember when I asked you if you knew of them, since you had the same last name?'

Cilla and Susan both looked. There appeared to be three generations in that family. And the eldest of them – a man and a woman – were looking at them intently, grins wide like a Cheshire cat's. Another younger couple turned to look as well.

As she felt Susan's hand tighten around hers, Cilla's heart almost jumped out of her ribs. Drew – the man who'd assisted her with her car, who'd waited on her at the restaurant – was among those Judy was pointing out. And when he smiled at her, she could not help the grin that formed on her own lips.

She turned to Susan to speak. But she found that Susan was now looking straight to the front, her eyes glazed. Susan dropped her hand just as the music team at the front began to lead them in praise.

Cilla looked back toward the other Robertson family. But they, too, were all now focused on singing. Cilla reminded herself why she was there and gave her full attention to the rest of the service.

Susan did well to concentrate that morning. The sermon was on Job, and she felt his pain most acutely. The preacher was speaking to her; he had to be. God was telling her something. He giveth and He taketh away. One day, Job woke up, the most prosperous man; and on the very same night he was poor and alone – his wife and children, as well as his wealth, all gone. Wasn't that the same for her? One moment, she had a loving husband and son going away for some much-needed holiday together; then, they were gone. Both taken from her so cruelly.

She almost cried as the preacher read the passage and then expanded on the topic of grief. But he did not end on Job's loss. He continued to explain God's sovereign hand in Job's story, His faithfulness and power. Nothing Susan hadn't heard before. But it struck a chord today. And she was caught off-guard, unprepared for her own well of tears spilling. Perhaps it was the setting. Perhaps it was the ambiance. Perhaps it was seeing John and Helen – and the past – suddenly so clear right in front of her eyes.

She spent the better half of the sermon looking down, letting teardrops trickle softly and clutching one of Cilla's hands. She felt a gentle nudge in her soul, but she wasn't ready to fully surrender. Yes, she knew the truth, but there was still a cold patch within her that she couldn't bear to part with. She was nursing her wounded heart, and she was afraid to let anyone – even Him – touch the torn and bruised parts. She was still too fragile.

When the service ended, Judy and Cilla thoughtfully allowed her some time to gather herself, not intruding with questions about how she enjoyed the service and so on. When she looked up at them, Cilla was excited.

'The family that Judy pointed out are coming our way.'

Susan's heart shot to a gallop. *Oh, Peter!* her heart wailed within.

'Do you know them? Do you think they're Dad's family?'

Susan opened her mouth to speak, but she was speechless. She hadn't expected to meet with them like this – so soon, unprepared. Her heart ached. Seeing Peter's relations brought back all the hurt of losing him all too soon. But hadn't she realised this was going to be the case? She was running from their life in Sydney, where everything reminded her of Peter and the life they had built for the past three decades, to ease the heartache. But she hadn't deeply considered that Orange was also still so much a part of their life as well. Sydney was their adult life. But Orange held the precious childhood and adolescent memories they shared; the growing up, the courtship, the memories of falling madly in love.

Before she could steady the beating of her heart, Judy's voice rang out. 'Hey, come meet my new friends!'

Susan turned to see John and Helen, Peter's second cousins, and their extended family almost across the aisle to their side. They were all smiles.

'Hi!' Helen was grinning ear to ear as she gave Judy a hug and kiss before turning to Susan. 'Susie!'

She sensed the minutest hesitation from Helen, so she stood and opened her arms to her. Without warning, another tear slid down her cheek. 'Damn this hay fever,' she chuckled as they continued to embrace. Helen didn't seem to want to let go, and Susan – or Susie, as she was called way back then – inexplicably felt the same way.

The crowd around them giggled when the hugging extended long enough.

Judy's jaw was on the floor. 'I'm missing something, right?'

Cilla grinned at her, a smidgeon of uncertainty in her eyes as well. 'Yes, I think I can explain some things. But …' She glanced at Andrew, who was lingering behind everyone else. 'Mum needs to explain a whole lot more.' She raised an eyebrow at Susan.

'Well, I'm sorry.' Helen moved away from Susan ruefully, her eyes now also teary. 'I mustn't hog you.'

As Susan turned to hug John, Helen shifted her attention to Cilla. 'And beautiful Priscilla, Susan's daughter-in-law.'

Susan watched as Cilla also teared up when Helen embraced her and patted her back. When the introductions were finished, one of John's grandchildren tugged at Susan's hand.

'Are you coming to have lunch with us?'

Susan looked down at the pretty, innocent face with ocean-blue eyes peering back at her.

Before Susan could register the question, John spoke up. 'Well, of course, you must!'

'It's my birthday, it's a family occasion!' one of John's sons added. Susan recalled he was the eldest. James, she remembered, going through the family tree in her mind. 'You have to come!'

She looked around at the expectant faces and laughed. 'I suppose we must, then, Cilla!' She grinned. 'We can't miss a family occasion. You didn't have any plans, did you?'

'I'm sure we only had afternoon naps scheduled on the calendar.' Cilla laughed and wrapped an arm around Susan's shoulders.

'Well, it's settled then.' John beamed as though he'd just discovered treasure.

As they headed toward the door, Susan couldn't shake the small knot in her belly. It had been three decades of little communication between her and Peter's relatives. Did they hold any grudges for their seeming snub of the country life? Did they think that their moving to Sydney also equated to turning their back on all their family and friends in Orange? At that time, so long ago, it was simply a yearning for an escape to something bigger … maybe better. In hindsight, she could understand if they all thought that she and Peter had cut them off. She was aware that Peter called his parents and wrote to a few of his cousins in the early days. But she had depended on him to keep the communication lines open and hadn't given it more thought. How inconsiderate she'd been! So young and naïve. She'd called and written to her side of the family infrequently. Now she wished she'd put more of an effort in keeping their connections. The heaviness of her guilt weighed on her mind.

As they stepped out into some sunshine, with the frigid air she remembered well of an early Orange winter, they all turned again to one another to exchange details of the get-together. She allowed Cilla to take charge of getting the directions from Judy as she quietly observed the others. John and Helen beaming at her; their grandchildren in a juvenile conspiracy of their own, chatting a little away from the adults; the children's parents having their own discussions; Judy's daughter typing on her phone. Susan's gaze finally landed on John and Helen's youngest, Andrew. And as she followed his gaze, she wasn't surprised to find his attention singularly on Cilla. Susan smiled and looked down when Andrew turned his eyes on her. As she looked at her feet, she recalled the bittersweet memory of another young Robertson looking with such admiration at Cilla. How she missed Michael right then.

Chapter 12

July.

Cilla stretched as she looked out the window, watching the last of the stubborn leaves fluttering softly to the ground, the trees' balding branches reaching up like skeleton fingers to the sky. Winter had undeniably moved in, blowing a chill wind most mornings the past week, but the kiss of sunshine penetrated the clouds to offer some comfort. The morning sun glazed her part of Orange with a golden glow.

Cilla had managed to convince her mother-in-law to attend church with her several weeks in a row. Susan seemed to have listened with quiet reflection to each sermon. They sat with Judy and her daughter and the Robertson family each Sunday and conversed with them afterwards.

At the lunch some weeks ago, she and Susan had a lovely time catching up with Peter's extended family, their connections being explained. Surrounded by her relatives, all doting on her, they were eager to hear about all that had happened, sympathising with their loss and expressing such joy in her return. And Cilla was welcomed as though they'd known her all her life.

Cilla was embarrassed to admit she could not recall meeting any of them prior to moving to Orange.

'At your wedding and…the funeral,' Helen softly explained.

'Oh.' Cilla had looked away quickly. 'I'm sorry I hadn't been more attentive.'

Helen had simply given her a hug. And Cilla felt the comfort of another mother.

As she drove with Susan to church again this morning, she reiterated how blessed she felt they were. That truly God's grace was following them; His mercies new every morning and His faithfulness great. And when their pastor recited the same verses in his sermon, Susan touched her hand and smiled. Cilla could see that while Susan maintained a reserved facade, her heart was beginning to thaw.

As she and Judy chatted outside in the sunshine after church, Cilla kept an eye on Susan interacting with John, Helen and the extended family.

She felt a gentle touch on her arm. 'How are you and Sue settling in?' Judy asked, no doubt also observing the group. 'Do you think she is comfortable here?'

Cilla kept her gaze on Susan. 'I ask her every week how she's going. She always answers in the positive. I try to engage her in a conversation about the sermon, and we have a nice little chat over lunch. But she doesn't talk much about her feelings about Peter and Michael. That kind of worries me,' she hesitated before continuing, 'because there was just this one occasion when she actually expressed how upset she was about having everything being taken from her. And I do wonder if she needs to have a good old, painfully honest conversation with God … you know?' She turned her gaze to Judy.

The other woman nodded. 'I do know what you mean. It's amazing of you to care so much for her and be with her at such a time like this.'

Cilla dipped her head. Her heart ached, too. 'Truth is, being with her is the only thing that seems to be keeping me sane.' She looked up, eyes wet. 'I … I need her, too. I miss Michael so much … and she …' Cilla suppressed a sob.

'Oh, darling.' Judy opened her arms and enveloped Cilla in a tight embrace. She patted her back gently. 'It's nice you have each other.'

'God has been really good to both of us,' Cilla replied into her comforter's shoulder, sounding muffled. 'Despite all that's happened, I know God cares for me and Mum. I'm so glad I still have her and that she let me tag along to Orange.'

Cilla heard gravel crunch as someone approached them and she broke away immediately to find a tissue from her bag.

'Oh, am I interrupting something?'

Judy answered for them. 'Hey, Boss. Just talking about how great God is to have reunited the best Robertson family in the world!'

Cilla turned around as soon as she'd wiped her eyes and nose to find Andrew, *their* boss – and, as it was made clear, not a guardian angel but her … *second-cousin-in-law? uncle?* – contemplating her with an uneasy smile. 'I'm sorry. I didn't mean to intrude on your conversation.'

Cilla gave him an assuring smile. 'Not at all. Just overwhelmed by the love of God, as Judy said.' And it was true that she felt that way. 'I feel like we've come home.' She chuckled. 'Well, *Mum* has come back home.'

Andrew's brows furrowed, though his smile remained intact. 'You … don't feel at home here?'

'Oh, no! That's not what I meant. I do feel at home. My home is where she is. I meant – she has literally come back home.'

Andrew nodded warmly, his smile wider. 'I get it.' He turned to look at his parents and siblings and their families. 'As long as my family is here, this is my home.' He turned to Judy. 'And how about you and Cassia – do you feel like Orange is your home now, too?'

'Oh, no question about it!' Judy laughed. 'I'm settled.'

'I'm glad.' Andrew's eyes shone. 'And I'm glad that working at the café is working out for both of you.' He glanced from Judy to Cilla. 'Well … I will see you both later.'

As he nodded and walked away, Judy sighed. 'He is such a nice man. Pity he doesn't have a family of his own. Yet.' She said the last word as though an afterthought.

Cilla found herself watching him as he moved on to chat with one of the ladies she'd seen on stage. 'I've kind of wondered about that,' she mused. 'But he seems content. And I've seen him with the violinist several times. I thought they were … together.' Realising she may be about to start gossiping, she changed gears. 'How old is our boss, anyway?'

'Not quite forty. Still young. But not so young, if you know what I mean.' She suddenly shifted. 'Oh, I forgot! I need him this week at the café. Sarah and Anton are both unavailable!'

'Really?' Cilla's pulse kicked up a notch. Having one of the waitresses out of action meant they were floored, but two workers at the same time was going to be challenging. Her hiring had proven timely, and she no longer doubted that she was needed. At times she'd even assisted with book-keeping. Judy had asked for her to help with some of the accounts when she was inundated with the month-end's paperwork. But, while waiting on tables was totally new to Cilla, she worked her heart out and made sure she was always welcoming to their customers.

'Both have some sort of cough or cold,' Judy explained.

'Must be the change in the weather,' they said together and laughed.

Judy nodded. 'Yes, that's what my mother always said. Blame it on the seasons. And there's meant to be some sort of alpine blast coming our way. Anyway ...' she motioned for her daughter, who was speaking to another lady, to follow her, 'I'd better talk to Drew. And here comes your family.' She motioned to Susan coming in their direction with John, Helen and another young man.

'Okay, bye.' Cilla hugged Judy back as her manager loped off to grab Andrew again.

Helen came to stand right next to her, arm draped over her shoulders in a motherly way. 'Susan and Cilla,' she introduced, 'this is Brian Munro. *Doctor* Brian.' She grinned at him. 'We've invited him and his sister to lunch. We'd love to have you and Susan as well. We've got to make up for lost time!' It sounded like a plea and her eyes shone with eagerness.

Cilla turned to Susan out of habit, and the slightest raise of her mother-in-law's eyebrows indicated her agreement. 'Sure,' Cilla answered for them.

As they chatted and walked leisurely to the carpark, she noticed Andrew finish his discussion with Judy. He headed toward the carpark, too, where he was joined by Maggie, the violinist. She wondered if they would also be joining them for lunch. She also wondered if there was romance blossoming for the Good Samaritan and the musician.

Chapter 13

Judy was right about pulling in Andrew to cover for Sarah and Anton. It wasn't without a hitch getting used to not having Sarah waiting on tables with her, but eventually Cilla found herself and the others settling into a rhythm taking orders, serving and cashiering. Her ankles felt the workout. Andrew also took some orders, but he was mostly in the back, preparing food with a baker and another cook. Cilla discovered he was even better than Anton at preparing the items on their menu.

'That's because he worked with his Mum and Dad when they owned the business,' Judy explained to her. 'He was here most afternoons after school and during weekends, helping his parents out, I've been told. If he hadn't made it big as an artist,' Judy confided, 'he probably wouldn't just own the place, he'd be running it himself.'

Cilla's eyes widened. 'He's an artist?'

Judy shook her head, looking frustrated. 'I can't believe we haven't covered this topic before.' She clicked her tongue. 'Just goes to show we've been flat out the last few months. Good for the business, though! *Anyway...*' Judy winked with a rueful smile. 'I like landscapes myself. But his big-time city clients seem to like all these abstract types of things he produces.' She giggled quietly. 'I don't know what I'm talking about. Maybe you like them, too. We have some hanging around here.'

Cilla's eyes grew even larger. 'Those paintings are his?'

Judy smirked and nodded. 'You like them, don't you?'

Cilla remembered the big canvases hanging on the walls around the café. One was a particular favourite, the one that had greeted her the first time she came through the doors. Something that looked like a vase with flowers, but done as a silhouette, smooth brushstrokes of mixed metallic paints with hints of pastel colours. It had made her feel ... embraced and invited, if a painting could produce such emotions. It was also one of those works that made you stand back and want to stare for hours.

'He was torn, he told me once,' Judy went on. 'He'd promised his parents he'd take the place over once they retired, but his art is a passion and he's done pretty well!'

'Surely his parents would have understood?' Cilla raised an eyebrow. 'And what about the other siblings?'

Judy shrugged. 'They each own their own businesses, a well-known family around here. That's why I asked if you knew them the first time we met, remember? Turns out, the story is bigger than that!' She waggled her eyebrows at Cilla. 'I can't believe he didn't say anything to me straight away. And to think – you had both already met!'

'I know!' Cilla laughed. 'I really don't remember meeting him at the funeral.'

Judy smiled sadly for her. 'Ah, my dear. You would have been in shock.'

'But then, for him to help me on the side of the road!' Cilla shook her head. 'I thought he was an angel of some sort, sent to help me out. And when I saw him here in the café when I was looking for a job, it was like a sign.'

An expression passed through Judy's face, but was gone before Cilla could think about it. 'Some sort of a coincidence, you think?'

Cilla shrugged. 'Coincidence seems like such a weak word, doesn't it? When this whole time, he's like my uncle or something!'

Judy scoffed. 'Your uncle! Ha! That is very funny.'

Cilla grinned. 'It is, isn't it! He would have been something like my husband's third-cousin.'

'A bit like the Filipinos, right?'

Cilla giggled.

Judy resumed brooming the floor behind the counter. 'I had a few Filipino friends back in Sydney. They called everybody cousins – even if they were second- or third-cousins – and aunties and uncles, even if some of them were younger!' She shook her head and they laughed. 'Anyway, two of Andrew's siblings are architects, working in partnership. Another one is the head chef of a restaurant in one of the vineyards. And Rachel, their only sister, is an accountant. They'd all married by the time Helen and John decided to retire. Except for Andrew. Still single. But he is managing both owning this and painting, er, *things*!' she chortled.

The man of talents, when asked to fill in, didn't hesitate to wash dishes, wipe tables and sweep floors. He covered every need Judy mentioned. He was well-presented and yet also seemed … *domesticated* was the word that popped into Cilla's head. He would have made a wonderful husband. And again, she wondered why he wasn't yet married. As it turned out, Maggie was Brian's sister, and they did join them for lunch last weekend. Perhaps it wouldn't be too long before their boss was married.

To Cilla, Andrew couldn't be more accommodating and personable. She'd been blessed with a considerate employer.

'Are you enjoying yourself here?' Andrew asked her at the end of her shift on Friday afternoon.

'Yes!' she eagerly responded. 'I'm learning a lot, Judy is amazing, and all the customers are so friendly. I'm loving Orange as well.'

Judy walked in then. 'Beats the city, doesn't it?'

'People seem so much more relaxed.' Cilla couldn't hide her pleasure. 'And of course, the food and company in here is great!'

'I'm glad Judy is looking after you.' Andrew turned to Judy, pleased. 'Make sure she gets take-aways, too. Enough for her and Sue.' Andrew winked at Cilla. 'Nothing like country air and country cooking!'

'I'm going to have a weight problem, the way everyone around here is feeding me!' Cilla patted her belly before she remembered she was already carrying more weight there. She ducked her head as she returned to wiping down the prep benches. She hoped Judy and Andrew did not notice her sudden embarrassment.

She heard Andrew give Judy some instructions and shortly Andrew was by her side with containers filled with food. 'Time to go home, young lady. Hope you and Sue enjoy some of these.'

Cilla looked at the boxes piled on top of each other – tarts, little merengues, macadamia brownie slices and mini cakes. And at the top of the four boxes, in brown paper bags, Cilla guessed were savoury pies.

She looked up at Andrew, surprised and unsure. She couldn't speak.

Judy stepped up to her, her eyebrows raised in concern. 'If you'd like something different, I could pack you something else? We've still got some quiche—'

Cilla let out a laugh. 'No, that's … this is great. I … I just hope Mum hasn't started on any dinner preparations!' Her eyes got a little misty, and she blamed it on hormones, hoping Andrew and Judy didn't notice. It wasn't time to tell them yet. And she didn't want to worry them about losing another worker. Not that she was irreplaceable. But she would give them all she had until she was legally obliged to tell her employers – and physically unable to work.

Chapter 14

Sipping her tea, Susan contemplated the snow outside as she sat in the warmth of her kitchen. That alpine blast and cold front the weather forecasters had been blathering on about in the news did finally arrive. The gray sky loomed angry directly above. It looked perfectly miserable out there and she wondered how Cilla was coping at work. She was only slightly showing her pregnancy despite being already six months along. And she hid her little bump well enough in her thick coats, black outfits and café uniform. Although anyone observing closely may well likely think she was beginning to take herself for granted, or – better yet – allowing herself to gain some healthy weight. She couldn't be persuaded to rest; young ones always thought they were invincible.

Susan sighed. Perhaps once the baby was born Cilla would finally slow down, stay home. She didn't mind the thought of looking after the baby every now and again if Cilla wanted to go out or find some *very* part time job if she wanted to.

But perhaps the young one still felt she needed to do more with her life. Susan was determined not to get in the way of that. She was exceedingly grateful that Cilla cared enough about her to follow her to Orange, to make sure she settled well in this almost-foreign place. And, through intuition, Cilla must have known she needed somebody these last seven months to keep her face looking up to their Saviour.

'You're so much stronger than me,' she murmured, still watching the rain. 'Precious Priscilla.' She could sense her deep sorrow, heard muffled sobs from her bedroom every now and again. But with her head held high, she glided through each day with vigour. Only lately had she taken to having naps on Sunday afternoons after lunch. She'd even gone out with some newfound friends from church, including the young doctor they met. He wasn't even trying to hide his keen interest in her.

Susan chuckled then. 'Get in line, Brian Munro.' The young doctor was always by Cilla's side at church since they'd been introduced a couple of weeks ago. He asked her many questions but talked mostly about himself and his medical ambitions. Bordering on monopolising her time, if Susan's opinion was asked.

She finished her tea and set about getting dinner ready. Cilla would be home soon, and she wanted her to sit and rest, put her feet up, maybe even have a quick nap. A nice roast would be just the perfect comfort meal for them. If she didn't get it started, Cilla would start it herself and force Susan to watch some boring quiz show and the news.

Soon enough, she heard the garage door squeak as it rolled up then down. Cilla appeared moments later.

'I think I'm tired.' Cilla dropped onto a dining chair with a huge sigh.

With concern, Susan made her a cup of tea, just as she knew Cilla liked. 'I'm surprised you're only just beginning to feel it. You've had a dream first pregnancy compared to some other women.'

'First?' Cilla echoed as she brought the cup to her mouth. She sipped the hot liquid and sighed, sounding weary.

Susan returned to her task of preparing dinner. 'Yes, first.' She ducked her head into the fridge and didn't hear Cilla's response.

When she rose up, she observed Cilla staring at a spot on the table, her mind obviously far away, hands wrapped around her warm cup.

Susan bit her lip. She shouldn't have made comparisons. 'I'm sorry, Cilla.' She wanted to kick herself. Of all the things to say to a first-time mother!

Cilla looked up. 'Why?'

Susan put the vegetables in her hands on the kitchen island. 'It's not nice to compare pregnancies. I should have known better. I wasn't thinking!'

'No, it's not that,' Cilla was quick to jump in. But she didn't elaborate, and Susan didn't want to prod.

After setting the oven to preheat, Susan cut the vegetables, occasionally throwing Cilla covert glances.

After some silence, Cilla finally spoke again. 'First and last.'

This time Susan trained her eyes on her. 'Don't say that.'

Cilla said no more but her pain was in that single tear that slid down her cheek. Susan's heart burst. She washed her hands, walked to Cilla and embraced her. Tight.

'You've got so much more ahead of you,' Susan soothed gently.

She felt Cilla shake her head against her shoulder. 'No, he's gone. Michael's gone.'

'There, there,' was all she could say. Her own wounds ripped open with the tears of her daughter-in-law. She remained quiet. There were no words that could bring their men back.

When she decided to speak, Susan was tentative with her words. 'You may … still …' she hesitated. Would it be okay to talk about future possibilities? She just wanted to give the girl some hope … without diminishing her loss. 'You've got time.'

Susan sighed, rubbing Cilla's back. She had to be compassionate but also – for both their sakes – realistic. 'Time may not heal all wounds. And I know it has only been some months. But … you've got so much love, girl, I know you do. There may be room there in your heart for … someone else. Sometime down the track.'

Cilla pulled back and shook her head. 'Mum! How could you say that?' She seemed taken aback by her own outburst and grabbed Susan's hand. 'I'm sorry. I didn't mean to be so rude. But I can't, Mum. I want Michael. I miss him so much.' More tears flowed. 'I – I … I just feel so tired.'

Susan nodded and helped her up. 'Come, come.' She led her to the couch and coaxed her to lay down and put her feet up. 'Of course you're tired, honey.' She shushed the rest of Cilla's protestations and swept the hair away from her face.

Susan kissed Cilla softly on the forehead as the young woman's eyes fluttered close. Susan got up and continued with dinner preparations, her heart heavy.

Chapter 15

August.

The dark mourning clothes still covered Cilla's pregnancy well. And the roomy blouses and thick winter coats she'd been wearing elsewhere had not elicited any remarks about expecting. But she couldn't deny that her energy drained more quickly. Her bump had also not grown much more. She had seen other women at six or seven months with protruding bellies and navels poking their dresses. But she'd only had to adjust the waist-tie on her café apron a little higher to accommodate her baby's growth. Even with her slight frame, she thought she would be showing a little more.

Her doctor was concerned and dissuaded her from working much longer.

'OK, I'll give them two weeks' notice.' Cilla's heart grew heavy at the thought of disappointing Judy and giving little time for her to find someone else. And as the weather changed again at the end of the month, more people would be coming to the café. More than that, she lamented the prospect of having little to do when she took on leave.

She was due in the last week of September, so she reasoned that it was probably time anyway. She really ought to get her head around preparing for the baby, with only eight weeks to go. Her only-slightly-pudgier middle hadn't given her away yet, but she wondered if some people were speculating about her weight-gain.

The next Monday, she was surprised to see Andrew come in. She wasn't aware of anyone being sick. She supposed it was just as well, so she could tell him and Judy at the same time. But her news could wait until the end of the day. The thought of letting them know both excited and unnerved her. She was convinced they would take it well, so her unease confused her. And it wasn't just an anxiety she felt in her chest, like an overwhelming emotion, she felt it in her belly and in her bones.

'Okay, who's sick?' she asked by way of greeting.

'Sarah is unwell. But, good morning to you!' Andrew cast her a glance that prompted a smile from her, making her forget her concerns for the time being.

'Good morning to you, too, Boss!' She'd taken to echoing Judy's affectionate title for him.

He grinned. 'You know I hate that!'

'Does Judy know?' She put her bag in a safe place in the kitchen and put on her apron. Again, she was conscious of carefully tying it a little higher and looser than when she first started.

Her pulse quickened a little. *Not yet, don't worry. You've got the rest of the day to think about how you're going to say it.*

'Of course, she does!' Andrew laughed. 'And that's why she keeps calling me that. But you've got no excuse. You, young lady, are much too sweet to be insulting anyone.'

If her face wasn't just thawing from being in the biting winter air outside, Cilla's cheeks would have burned. She turned away to pick up a cleaning spray and cloth.

Get a grip. What is wrong with you today? It's just a simple compliment.

Relieved to hear Judy's voice announce her arrival, she escaped from the kitchen and worked her way through the tables in the dining room, pulling down chairs and wiping tabletops with a little more vigour than usual.

A wave of nausea hit her. *Just nerves. Big day today.*

Right on six am, patrons began to arrive to get their hit of caffeine, breakfast and sugar. Cilla welcomed the busyness, completely occupied with pleasing her customers and distracted from her thoughts.

The nausea lingered, though. By the lull after ten am, when most of the workers and students had disappeared into their offices and schools, Cilla became more aware of her dizziness and a dull ache in her abdomen. While there was no one at the register, she turned to the kitchen to find Judy.

But she saw Andrew first. Or rather, Andrew saw her. 'Cilla, what's wrong?'

'Sorry?' Cilla looked up at him, feeling a little dazed. He seemed to be vignetted in a circle of gray.

Andrew ran to her. 'You're so pale! What's wrong?'

Aware that she'd fallen into Andrew's arms, she was embarrassed at the state she was in. 'I think I need to sit down.' Her lower back also ached.

'Oh, my goodness! What's wrong?' Judy's shrill voice came from somewhere behind her. 'Cilla!'

'I think I just need a little time out to sit.'

Anton's voice piped in. 'I think you need an ambulance.'

'No …' Cilla's protest was weak as she tried to push up from Andrew's arms. 'Maybe water and something to nibble on.'

'Are you diabetic?' Andrew asked.

No, I'm pregnant, she wanted to say but didn't feel it was the right time to discuss that maternity leave. She shook her head instead.

'Anemic?' Judy pushed strands of Cilla's hair from her face.

Without warning, a pinching pain caused Cilla to gasp.

'OK, that's it.' Andrew's grip around her tightened. 'I'm taking you to emergency.'

'No, I'll be fine.'

'I'm not giving you a choice in the matter.'

At the urgency in Andrew's voice, it dawned on her that not only was she in danger, but the aches and nausea may be her baby's way of getting her attention.

Oh, God, it's too early! Please don't let me have a miscarriage. This baby is all I've got left of Michael!

She stifled a sob at the thought of him. Panic set in. She didn't want to lose this baby. She didn't want to lose Michael all over again.

Chapter 16

*H*e *would make a good son-in-law,* Susan mused. But there were a few hurdles to jump. One was the fact that he was practically family.

But not our blood relation, she objected against her own reasoning.

Secondly, Cilla was most definitely not even thinking about dating. She was still grieving, still so heartbroken. It was too soon.

She swept the curtain to one side to look out her bedroom window. There was no snow, but a light shower was falling on their barren front lawn.

Aren't you *still grieving for your husband?* she chided herself. Of course, it would take time to get over the love of one's life. And would she want her own son to be replaced so soon?

No, she conceded. But she felt greatly convinced that it would be good for Cilla to love again. To be loved by someone who was so clearly captivated by her. But whether Cilla was ready was not for her to decide or interfere with. Despite her struggle with her own faith, she still believed – if not currently felt – that God was in control of both her and Cilla's lives.

She chuckled, remembering that Cilla seemed quite oblivious to the small number of men watching her with keen interest. One of them, at least, had more than enough confidence to continually engage her at his every opportunity. Some, too shy to start even a conversation. And one other, keeping himself relatively casual, tentative, and seemingly more unsure than Susan herself how Cilla would respond.

'Just make a move,' she muttered, her eyes not really seeing their sad front lawn. 'Take a risk. Do what you've got to do. Slow and steady.'

Susan trudged to the warm kitchen. Cilla always left the heating set to a toasty temperature in the cold winter mornings of Orange that they were now getting accustomed to.

She made herself a cup of coffee. Ah, that hit the spot. There was a sausage breakfast muffin covered with clear wrap sitting on a plate on the island and a note on it from Cilla instructing her to 'just heat it in the microwave.'

When her cousins visited a little later for tea and a craft session, she vaguely raised the subject of Cilla and all the possibilities churning in her mind.

Frances, who was knitting Cilla a crimson scarf, nodded in sympathy. 'Yes, young love is the best. We all know that.' She looked around at the other three women with her, all of them had married in their early twenties. 'Losing someone so early would have been devastating for her. She probably thinks she can never love again.'

'But, on the other hand, the young ones are resilient,' Mary piped in. She didn't know how to knit or sew, so she came just for the chats and the tea. 'She'll recover from the heartache. She'll love Michael forever, sure. But that doesn't mean she can't love again.'

Susan nodded. 'That's what I've been trying to tell her. But you know, I don't want to seem pushy.' She counted the loops in the square she was crocheting and continued. 'When I tried to talk to her about it, I made her cry. I'm scared to bring it up again. The thing is …' She hesitated and looked around at the ladies, pondering how much she should say.

When she remained silent a second too long, the other ladies stopped.

Connie, her needle paused over her embroidery, gazed pointedly over her glasses at Susan. 'What is it, Sue?'

Susan sighed and decided to spill. 'Well … it's probably no surprise – she's an attractive young lady – that there are already a few guys interested in her.'

Mary laughed, sounding relieved. 'I thought you were going to tell us something bad!' She put her cup and saucer down on the coffee table and leaned forward. 'I can tell you, I've visited the café often enough and seen a few young guys who seem very friendly with her. I can understand that. She's very nice, very engaging, always has a smile for all the customers.'

'But there are a few at church who may be particularly interested in her,' Susan said slowly, carefully choosing her words. 'And I wonder if she is aware of how they are feeling about her, and if she will – or should – start dating again.'

'I think that will take some time,' Frances said, also returning to her knitting. 'Perhaps she knows they're interested in her.'

'If she realises that, and if she's not ready to do so, then she shouldn't be so friendly with them,' Susan reasoned, 'as they may get the wrong idea.' Dr Munro came to mind. She sighed. 'Unfortunately, Cilla *is* naturally friendly. Even through the course of her relationship with Michael, she was friendly with everyone. The difference was, everyone *knew* she was Michael's girlfriend, then fiancée, then *Missus Dr Robertson* and there was no mistaking that she was totally besotted with him and him alone. As friendly as she was, no one held a candle to Michael. This time around, she's holding herself up so well, you would never catch her grieving – except me, because I sometimes hear her crying in her bedroom—'

At this, the other ladies clicked their tongues and shook their heads. 'Tsk, tsk. Poor girl,' they muttered.

Susan put her wool and needle down and considered how much more she should share. Her silence concerned the girls.

'What are you not telling us?' Mary was looking at her with a smirk on her face. 'After all these years – decades – you still have this look on your face that makes it so obvious there's something else you want to say.'

Susan bit her lip and leaned back in her chair. 'There *is* one I am particularly concerned about.' She hesitated, looked up at the ceiling, then looked at each of the ladies.

Each of the faces staring back at her clearly said, *Who?* and possibly, *get on with it!*

'Andrew Robertson.'

Frances and Connie both opened their mouths to say something, and Mary quickly swallowed the tea she'd just sipped. 'Drew?' she repeated. 'Your husband's dad's cousin's son?'

The ladies burst out laughing.

'Yes, the very one.'

Still chuckling, Frances resumed her knitting. 'So, what's wrong with him? Nice young man. Why he's still a bachelor, I don't know. I thought young ladies liked the free-spirited, arty-type these days.'

'Probably got hurt by a previous relationship,' said Mary.

'Men are too picky and fickle these days,' added Connie. 'And they think they can procreate until they're in their eighties, that's why they're marrying later!'

'Maybe he just hasn't met the right one! Maybe he's got high standards. Who knows!' Mary waved a dismissive hand. 'And anyway, he's got that café as well, doesn't he? I've seen him working there sometimes. Maybe he's been keeping himself busy. Minding his *own* business.' She chuckled. 'Not like us!'

'But it's exactly what Connie said,' Susan reasoned, ignoring their musings. 'He's family. We're related. Won't it seem a bit … odd?'

'Why?' asked Frances. 'Does it seem odd to you?'

'It's far enough removed, I think,' said Mary.

'And he's certainly not related to Cilla,' added Connie.

Susan sighed. 'I know ...' She picked up her crocheting, though not really seeing it. 'I'm not even related to them, either. But they've taken us in like family, even Cilla. John and Helen just embraced us as though no years have passed, as though Peter is still alive. They treat Cilla as if she's *my* own daughter.'

'And you think Andrew is interested in her in more than just a second-cousin-thrice-removed sort of way?' Connie chortled.

Susan nodded.

'Oh, Susie! That's wonderful!' Mary clapped her hands. Susan could sense the cupid in her beginning to wake.

'Yes, but, remember,' Susan cautioned them, 'Cilla may not necessarily want his – or anyone else's – attention right now.'

'Well, maybe we can help things along.' Frances' smile was conspiratorial.

'Ladies, I don't want to mess with her. She's so precious to me. I don't want her to get

hurt, especially as she's just endured so much…
And there's Maggie. There are ladies at church
who've been praying for her and Drew.'

Susan's phone buzzed and they all jumped.
As the other ladies giggled and chatted quietly,
presumably coming up with an elaborate match-
making plan, Susan answered the call.

'What? Where?' she asked with urgency,
stopping the chatter of her cousins. 'We'll be
right there.' She hung up and picked up her bag.

She summoned them to the door
impatiently. 'Come on, ladies. Cilla's in hospital.'

Chapter 17

The steady heartbeat from the monitor was a comforting sound to Cilla. She sighed, relaxing her head and shoulders on the pillow. Now that she was settled in a room, she wondered how Andrew had fared looking for parking. He'd dropped her off in Emergency and ensured she was with a nurse before he moved his car from the five-minute drop-off zone.

He had not returned to her since, and she'd already had an ultrasound and a brief interview with a nurse. After what seemed like ages, alone in the room with only the bleeping of monitors, another nurse poked her head into the room to make a quick announcement.

'Mrs Robertson, your husband is waiting outside. We've just buzzed him in. I'll be back with some pain killers the doctor prescribed for you.'

She was gone before Cilla could correct her. Horrified that Andrew had been mistaken for Michael, she stared at the ceiling, wishing so badly that Michael was there right now, holding her hand, comforting her, stroking her belly and speaking to their baby. But instead of feeling comforted by her thoughts of Michael, her chest tightened as desire for his presence engulfed her.

Before she could sink further into her emotional abyss, there was a soft knock on the door. Andrew's smiling face came into view.

'Well, go in. Don't be shy.' The nurse's voice came from behind him. She peeked around Andrew's broad shoulders and waved. 'I'll leave you two alone, but I'll check back regularly.' And with that, she zoomed away again.

Despite the awkward silence, with Andrew standing by the door, her nerves calmed down. Peace began to engulf her, a sense of gratitude pushing away some of her distress. She waved her hand to invite him closer. 'Thank you for getting me here.'

'You're welcome.' He looked uncertain. 'I guess ... congratulations are in order?'

Heat rushed to Cilla's face. 'I'm sorry, I was going to tell you soon. Today, actually.'

He asked how far along she was, and his expression made her laugh when she admitted she was due the very next month.

'I never would have guessed.' Tentatively, as though the space between them was fragile, he stepped even closer. 'You need to take leave. Immediately.'

She began to protest. 'No! I'm giving you at least two weeks' notice. Aren't I supposed to do that?'

Andrew shook his head and smiled in assurance. 'No. You should be looking after yourself and your baby. Waiting on tables, on your feet the whole day ... I don't want you exerting yourself.' Frustration filled his eyes.

Cilla turned her head to the monitors. The speech she'd prepared was out the window. 'I didn't want to disappoint you. Or spring this on you. Now you're going to have to find someone quickly.'

Andrew choked. 'Are you kidding me? How could you possibly disappoint me because of this?' He came even closer, now right by her bed. 'The café is the last thing you should be thinking about. That's my problem to sort.' His tone softened. 'Actually, it's Judy's problem.' When she turned her head back to him, there was laughter in his eyes.

'The nurse said I'm doing fine. Just a false alarm. Nothing to worry about. If you don't mind, I'd like to work at least two more weeks.' Her eyes sought his approval. 'Please.' She willed back the wetness that had suddenly glazed her eyes. She didn't want to be a cry-baby. Not in front of her employer.

Oh, Michael. She closed her eyes and wished him next to her. But she knew it was a useless exercise. So she opened her eyes and focused on the man who *was* beside her, looking down with such obvious concern and compassion.

She was grateful. Grateful that he had insisted on taking her to the hospital. That there was someone caring for her in her distress when her own husband couldn't be there, and when she hadn't been paying attention to her own body.

The too-calming comfort of his presence sent a jarring echo through her chest. *Don't go overboard. He is not your husband and he is not a substitute for Michael.*

I just feel so lonely, Lord. I feel so alone. Again, she leaned back and looked to the ceiling.

'Cilla!' Susan's voice snapped into her consciousness and she was grateful for the arrival of her mother-in-law. Hot on her heels were Aunts Frances, Connie and Mary, and she smiled at them. All would be well now, she knew.

As the ladies fussed, it didn't go unnoticed to her that Andrew quietly slipped out of the room.

Chapter 18

The realisation that Cilla felt rather *too* comfortable with Andrew by her bedside at the hospital made her feel *very* uncomfortable.

Susan and her three cousins had taken her home when the doctor gave her the all-clear. Just false contractions, the gynecologist assured, severe though they may have felt. But the baby was fine and certainly not yet ready to make an entrance. Or, rather, an exit.

The doctor and the midwife who had checked her were visibly confused about Andrew's identity, seeing as he brought her to the hospital and shared the same last name. In the car, Aunt Frances giggled about them referring to Andrew as her husband. At first, Cilla had laughed. But the butterflies that flitted up from her belly to her chest were not due to the baby's quickening. This feeling was something else. And the memory of his intense gaze was unsettling. It bore into her fragile soul, exposed her needs.

She decided to take everyone's advice to lay down for the rest of the afternoon.

With unsolicited thoughts taunting her, she relented and agreed to stop working at the café immediately. Her feelings continued to bother her over the following days, and guilt settled in as she thought about Andrew more often since the incident.

Just because he looked after you and was there at the hospital doesn't mean he's interested in you any other way. And for goodness' sake, you've just lost your husband! You're grieving! You just want Michael to be with you, sharing the joy of this beautiful gift with you! Instead, there was someone else who just happened to be there, and you're just grateful. What you need is someone who loves you, cares for you because he wants to be with you. Not someone who pities your situation.

Similar reflections troubled her over the following weeks. Surely the looks he gave her were looks of sympathy, no more. And the flutters she felt at the kindness of his tone, the softness of his touch – nothing but her hormones. She continued to attend church and show Andrew the same respect as always, although toned down her friendliness markedly. Eventually, everyone who knew her finally learned she was pregnant. The extended Robertson clan were obviously very pleased for her, as though all of them were comforted that Michael had left his legacy. A bittersweet situation. But Maggie's brother, Brian Munro, who had been her most attentive companion, seemed to distance himself.

The next time she bumped into Brian, his demeanour was markedly changed.

'How are you going?' She was bright and chirpy in her greeting.

'I'm well,' he answered. His smile no longer held its usual warmth. 'Yourself?'

'I'm well, too.'

His brief response was awkward. He had usually engaged – even manipulated, she admitted – her time most other occasions they were thrown together. She'd entertained his attentions because she didn't want to be rude, and he seemed to have appreciated her attentiveness to him.

Dr Munro put his hands in his jacket pockets to warm them. 'I heard about your news. Congratulations.'

'Thank you,' she answered, surprised at his cool tone. 'Getting close now,' she decided to add.

'Hmm.' He looked away. 'I'm going back to Sydney. I've got a fantastic opportunity waiting for me because one of my contacts just bought a practice in Bondi. Great location.'

Cilla clapped her hands together. 'Fantastic! Congratulations.' She moved to hug him, but he made no indication that he was going to meet her halfway. She caught herself and clasped her hands in front of her instead.

Brian regarded her as though he couldn't quite believe she was truly happy for him. 'Thanks.'

'You must be excited.' She smiled with sudden uncertainty.

'Of course.'

She opened her mouth to say more, but Brian's usual playfulness was not present. Instead, he looked uncomfortable, even uninterested. He mumbled a bland goodbye and turned as she waved. Had she offended him? Or did the knowledge of her being pregnant make him uncomfortable? She pushed away her negativity, unwilling to add to the other worries she already nursed.

But the thoughts she couldn't dismiss were of Andrew Robertson. She'd caught him looking at her now and again. She wondered if he had read her mind during those times she'd had *irregular* thoughts about him, about feeling *feelings* for him – feelings she shouldn't have. Feelings a pregnant, newly-widowed woman shouldn't entertain. All the more reason to be on guard over her heart and mind!

Yes, he had become a great friend to her, was always kind to her, sent her and Susan food every so often with either Judy or Cassia or one of the other waiters, but nothing so outrageous that should make her think he favoured her.

And when it seemed all the older women around her constantly spoke highly of Andrew, his character, his amazing paintings, how great he was and so on, it was hard not to think of him.

Now that she was home every day, she received more visitors from church, the café and extended family. And all they seemed to want to talk about was Andrew, Andrew and Andrew. Was she being paranoid? Or were they deliberately talking about him in her presence, even if the conversation did not include her? Perhaps, *she* was the one noticing his name mentioned more often than usual.

She was beginning to resent it.

Chapter 19

Susan perceived the melancholy turn in her daughter-in-law's mood of late. 'Cilla?'

Cilla looked up from folding laundry, her eyes wide. 'Hm?'

What scenarios had she interrupted in the young lady's mind?

'I can tell you've got lots of things spinning up here—' she pointed to her temple, 'and I know you well enough to see that you're quite bothered.'

They both needed to be truthful with each other, if not transparent.

Transparent?

A cautionary bell went off in her head. She wasn't exactly being entirely transparent with all the ideas in her own mind. But she had to be careful. Careful with a lot of things, particularly when it came to matters of the heart.

Cilla looked at Susan under her lashes, hesitated to speak, then looked away. Far away. When she turned her face back to Susan, she had a single tear slowly making its way to her chin. Susan felt at a loss.

'Talk to me,' she encouraged, her voice soft.

Cilla swiped the tear away, impatient with herself. 'Please don't judge me,' she pleaded.

Susan shook her head, concerned. 'I wouldn't – what do you mean?'

Cilla gave way to a few more tears. 'I have these ... unwanted feelings.'

Her pulse quickening, Susan forced herself to sound nonchalant. 'Yes?'

Cilla turned away, looked out the kitchen window at the blackness outside. She groaned, exasperation evident. 'Andrew. His name just seems to be popping up in every conversation.'

Susan swallowed. 'And that ... that bothers you?'

Cilla didn't respond for a time. She kept her gaze averted. Eventually, she shrugged, looking helpless. 'It does. And I don't know why.' She shook her head. 'Well, maybe I do know – I mean, I think it bothers me because …' She broke a little, looked at Susan with what seemed like guilt, and forced herself to continue. 'I – I feel terrible, Mum.'

Motherly instinct kicked in, but Susan stopped herself from going to Cilla straight away to comfort her. She wanted to hear her thoughts. 'About what?'

'I – I've … Thoughts of him have been plaguing my head.' She looked mortified. 'Ever since the hospital thing. When he helped me. And found out about the baby.' Her sentences clipped, she went on, 'Maybe I just want Michael. I needed Michael there, but instead Andrew was there. This is *Michael's* baby! *He* should have been there! … Oh, Michael!' she wailed then, looking away and clutching tea towels to her chest. 'I don't want anybody else!'

Her heart also breaking, Susan looked away as a tear dropped to her hand. She needed to be strong for Cilla, but she couldn't deny the pain that a mother's shattered heart felt. She missed her son deeply, but the young widow's anguish reverberated in her bones.

After a time, Cilla's sobs turned to soft tears until, finally, they both sat in silence. Susan decided it was a good time for caffeine. She got up and started the machine. 'I need coffee. I'll make you a hot chocolate.'

Cilla sniffed. 'Thanks, Mum.' She stretched out on the sofa, the folding of laundry forgotten, and pulled a throw over her.

When Susan handed her the mug, she caught her hand. 'Please, Mum. Don't tell anyone about this.' Cilla's eyes were wide, pleading.

Susan promised without a second thought.

Cilla's expression turned to gratitude. 'I couldn't bear it if anyone found out. Especially Andrew. It would be too embarrassing.'

'Embarrassing?'

Cilla looked away. 'I'm so hormonal, I don't know what to feel. Sometimes, I feel so happy about this baby. Sometimes, I feel so sad because Michael's not here to share this joy with me. I just want to cry and feel so sorry for myself. And then, there have been a few times – I'm   so

embarrassed to admit – that I've wondered if …'
She shook her head, her sentence unfinished.

Susan hazarded a guess. 'Andrew?'

'I'm so ashamed. I feel so guilty. How could someone else take the place of Michael so soon in my mind. Isn't that terrible? *I'm* terrible for even thinking about someone else. I know Andrew's just a really nice person. And he's kind of family, so he treats us so.'

'Well … not directly,' she added softly, even though she knew it wasn't the issue.

'I've just lost my husband! I'm still in mourning. How could I even entertain the thought of any other man, just because he's been so nice to me? Just because he was there at the hospital when my husband wasn't.'

'Well, he's always so attentive to us,' Susan conceded softly, knowing she probably wasn't really helping. 'He really is just a decent human being.'

'That's right! You're absolutely right! Maybe he just feels sorry for me.'

Susan shrugged, not entirely in agreement. 'We-ell … he has been extra kind.'

'And he and Maggie would make a great couple. They're together, right?'

'I really don't think so.'

Again, after some silence, she spoke. 'Can we please not discuss him again?'

'Of course.'

In the days following, Susan noticed the mantles, shelves and other available tabletops begin to fill with photographs. Michael with Susan and Peter. Michael with Cilla at his graduation. His twenty-first birthday. Their wedding; their honeymoon. Michael as a teenager; his baby photos…

Michael was in every room.

Chapter 20

Something deep within Cilla snapped. Like the flick of a rubber band. Her instincts told her something was very wrong. 'No! Not yet!' She inhaled sharply.

It was the coldest time of the morning. Cilla bolted upright and pushed all her covers to one side of her bed, temperature a non-consideration. She breathed deeply, tuning in to the sensations in her body, fighting to control the panic threatening to overwhelm her. She felt the tightening in her belly. This time, it wasn't a practise contraction. It was more intense than the ones that sent her to the hospital the first time.

'Mum!' she called in as calm a tone as she could manage. She made it just in time into the tiled bathroom, water flowing from her like a bouquet of burst water balloons. 'Su-san!'

Susan was in the hallway without delay, looking alert despite having been rudely awakened just then. 'Cilla, oh my goodness!'

Cilla gasped as another contraction peaked. Holding back a groan, she grabbed her mother-in-law's hand and looked to her for strength. 'I think it's time.' She didn't want to voice out her only anxious thought: it was six weeks too soon.

Susan nodded and started talking. Cilla was in a blur. She heard Susan give instructions as she walked around the kitchen, pulling things out of drawers, the fridge, the cupboards, and stashing them in a cooler bag.

Cilla forced herself to maintain deep breathing as another contraction came. She checked the time: *four minutes*. She showered quickly, pulled on her preprepared hospital outfit and her thickest coat, and met her mother-in-law in the front room. Susan held her maternity bag, long ready for this moment.

'Anything else you want to take to the hospital?'

Cilla shook her head. She wanted for nothing more than her mother-in-law to get her to the hospital. She wanted to get down on her hands and knees and push. Instead, she headed to the door. The blast of cold air greeted her even before it was half open, but the sun was faithfully in its place, promising to bring some warmth.

She remembered one of the first verses she memorised: *For I know the thoughts that I think toward you, says the Lord, thoughts of peace and not of evil, to give you a future and a hope.*

His voice was loud and clear, providing her His peace. But Cilla didn't have a chance to ponder all its weight and depth at that very moment, even as she recited the verse over and over in her mind. She simply wanted Michael's baby to be okay.

Zane Michael Robertson took a mere sixty-seven minutes to announce his arrival with a hearty cry after Susan got Cilla to the hospital. When Cilla passed the wrapped bundle into her arms, the remaining icicles hanging onto Susan's heart melted. And when the baby opened his eyes and looked as though he was studying his grandmother's face, she found herself falling in love again.

Chapter 21

September.

When the excitement of the new Robertson baby calmed a little, and the toys arriving daily with the visitations of friends and church family began to trickle down from its original downpour, Susan surveyed their home. There were toys, big and small, in the lounge room and the three bedrooms. And the larger ones – like the electric car – were in the garage. Clothes were piled everywhere, more than enough for each stage of baby's growth spurt over the next two years – for cold and warm seasons. Likely, he wouldn't get to wear all of them before Cilla would have to give them away. *Or put them aside*, Susan hoped.

She quietly observed that Andrew visited often, both with his family as well as on his own over the first few weeks after Zane was born. Susan could see his concern. And if she was not mistaken, she observed a strong affection for Zane from the outset. The way he looked at Cilla, too, made Susan's own romantic heart flutter. She wished Cilla would see it.

On the contrary, while she witnessed clearly that Cilla was nothing but the most polite to all her guests, she was visibly reserved in her behaviour towards Andrew.

'Here!' Susan passed the baby to Andrew. 'Hold Zane. I want to take a photo of you together!'

While Cilla watched from a recliner in the other corner of the room, resting, Susan stole a glance in her direction. She noted the young woman's wistful countenance.

Susan sighed. *God, where to from here?*

It hadn't been enough that Michael's photographs were on tables and mantles and bookshelves. Framed pictures of Michael now hung on the walls, too. There was no chance Cilla – or anyone – could walk anywhere in their home without seeing his handsome, boyish face either smiling his serious doctor smile or grinning with mischief as a teenager with his friends. Her favourite wedding photo, enlarged and framed after their honeymoon, hung on Cilla's bedroom wall right where she would see it the moment she opened her eyes in the mornings. Other wedding photos taken with family and friends were in smaller frames and adorned some of their shelves. His childhood albums and their photobooks were piled on the coffee table in the lounge room.

Michael was everywhere for all their visitors to see. And she believed that was the way Cilla wanted it.

October.

Susan was reluctant to leave Cilla alone, but the young woman had insisted she would be *fine* and that Susan should still go to church. She felt she ought to go, but also felt a tinge of guilt leaving Cilla alone not feeling the best.

'It would just be a couple of hours. I'll be fine, I'm just staying in bed. Zane's within easy reach.' Cilla practically pushed her out the door.

She wondered if Cilla was avoiding certain people – or a certain *someone* – since several people had called in during the week, and she had entertained them all except Andrew. When he came to visit, she asked Susan to apologise for her, saying her back was aching and she felt nauseated so she didn't feel like she could get out of bed. Of course, Susan didn't question Cilla, and Andrew was courteous enough to instead have a brief catch up over coffee with her before leaving. He also didn't let on about the glaringly obvious Michael-themed décor of their home, bless him!

Susan sighed as she stepped out of the car in the church's parking lot, grateful for the warmer weather, and asked God to help her stop worrying about her daughter-in-law. *She's in your hands, Lord.*

She shut her door and locked it. As she walked towards the front entrance, she muttered a prayer. 'Please give me wisdom. Show me when I need to butt out of other people's business but *do* prompt me loud and clear when I must say or do something.'

'Susan!'

She almost cried out in surprise when she heard her name. Deep in prayer as she walked, she was unaware of the people around her.

'Didn't mean to frighten you.' Andrew approached her with a smile.

She smiled back. Her heart, she realised, was growing ever softer towards him each time they met. He was like a balm that soothed her yearning for her son. 'Hi, Drew. Running late today? That's unusual.'

Andrew glanced at his watch. 'Two minutes to spare. How are you?'

'I'm well.' Susan was sure Andrew was itching to know how Cilla was. 'And, no, Cilla wasn't feeling well this morning.' Before he could ask, she assured him that it wasn't her back that was still troubling her. 'She just wasn't feeling a hundred per cent. Hormones and all that. Body having to adjust with baby's needs, you know …'

'I see.' He beckoned to her. 'Sit with us.'

'Of course.'

As they sat with the rest of the Robertson clan and with Judy and her daughter, they asked about Cilla, clearly concerned that she still wasn't up to coming to church since she'd given birth. Susan gave them the same explanation she had just given Andrew, almost word for word.

The musicians at the front were taking their place on stage when Andrew looked down at her with sincere concern in his eyes. 'Is she really okay?'

Susan opened her mouth to assure him again, but the musicians started playing. Andrew turned to the front, but not before she saw a flash of doubt in his expression. She gathered he wasn't really expecting to get a straightforward answer to his question. They would need to talk after the service.

As the pastor spoke about God's call on Jeremiah, Susan couldn't help but wonder what of God's plans were left for her and Cilla. Though she still wanted to question God on the reasons why He took her husband and son so early, she could not escape the hope that was beginning to well in her heart.

Andrew was patient to wait for everyone who wanted to chat after the service. Eventually, though, people went separate ways and Andrew asked Susan again about Cilla.

'Is she recovering well, Susie? Is there anything else that she's concerned about? Anything I can help with?'

Susan studied him as she contemplated what she should and shouldn't say. There was no use ignoring the obvious. Andrew's affections for Cilla were clear as a summer day. *Did his family know about it?* she wondered. Although he was very careful with his actions, he wasn't exactly covert either.

'Perhaps.' It was the best answer she could give him. She knew – or thought she knew – what was bothering Cilla. But she had also promised her not to speak of this particular matter again. Specifically, Cilla had made it clear that she didn't want to speak of the possibility of a relationship with Andrew.

'Perhaps?' Andrew stuffed his hands in his pockets. 'Sue, you know her better than anyone, so I trust whatever you say. But if either of you are in need of anything, and it's in my power to do something, please let me know. I really want to help.'

Susan looked away. She may have promised Cilla not to speak about Andrew again but she had made no promises about speaking *to* him. Was that a valid loophole?

She turned back to Andrew. 'It's a bit too bright out here. Shall we have a proper chat somewhere else? Not too long. Cilla's expecting me home after church.'

Despite the concern still in his eyes, Andrew's smile was painted with relief. 'A proper chat sounds good. And, no, I won't take up too much of your time.'

For the briefest instant, Susan felt a sense of déjà vu. It wasn't too long ago when she and her son used to have spontaneous chats over coffee at randomly selected cafes. The memories threatened to squeeze the breath out of her lungs, and she pushed them away. Bittersweetly, she chose to focus instead in the moment. There was another man's heart at stake.

Chapter 22

November.

Cilla thought she would be restless with inactivity after giving up work. She was restless, all right! Besotted with her newborn and learning to care for him, her new-mother's heart was all in. Entertaining well-meaning visitors had kept her mind from wandering to thoughts she had previously wrestled with. And it was Michael on her mind during sleepless nights.

But life settled down again for Cilla. When the guests dwindled down to just the aunts and the Robertsons taking it in turns to visit, Andrew was markedly absent. She allowed herself to wonder where he was.

In truth, she missed his friendship. She missed the easy way they had related to each other. Oh, if only her feelings hadn't got in the way! If only she didn't long for Michael so much.

The Christmas season came early for the two women. Susan cannot be helped with her sudden shopping impulses. Baby clothes, toys and accessories began to pile up in the only bedroom they had left free. It was supposed to be a little office or computer room. Up until the baby shower, it had been a storage room for the nick-nacks they were yet to unpack. Now, those things were in the garage.

'Mum, you must stop!' Cilla laughed after Susan came home one day with a cute rocking horse.

Susan's eyes widened at her. 'What?' She was all innocence. 'I'm going to put it away for when he's older. He's not going to get spoiled with toys all in one go!'

Cilla rolled her eyes and giggled some more. 'I don't know who you think you're fooling! This kid is already beyond spoiled, and he doesn't even know it yet.'

The closet in the third bedroom was filled with baby clothes, flowing in during Zane's first few weeks. Aunts Frances, Connie and Mary were very generous with what they could knit, crochet as well as purchase, all ogling the precious new prince in their midst. Cots and change-tables came generously from the other Robertson family – John and Helen, and their children. And, of course, there was the gorgeous painting that Andrew's sister had commissioned him to paint especially for the baby. Although it wasn't *from* Andrew himself, his handiwork had him imprinted all over it.

She sighed. Denying thoughts of him was futile. He had left a month ago on a business trip, and she hadn't seen him, hadn't heard where he was or what he was doing. It was as though he'd disappeared, but for the fact that an envelope was handed to her by Rachel some weeks later. There wasn't much more than the word 'Congratulations' on it, but he'd parted with a very generous amount on the gift card. She tried to get in touch to thank him, but he was unreachable. His family could only say he was on a special project and also didn't know how to reach him. She wondered if Maggie would know. And if she did, then it was none of Cilla's business.

'It's rather odd, isn't it?' she mused. It was a warm afternoon in late November, and Cilla and her mother-in-law sat in the quiet of their lounge room. Susan knitted as Cilla nursed Zane.

Susan looked up from her knitting. 'What's odd, love?'

Cilla sighed, hesitated. Did she really want to bring up the topic of Andrew? She shook her head at Susan. 'Nothing. Never mind.' Perhaps, he would come home at Christmas. Surely, he would want to be with his family at that time. And what about Maggie? He wouldn't be away from her too long. She and Andrew were not-so-secretly being matched. She wouldn't want her to think she was competing for Andrew.

Another reason why she ought to stop thinking about Andrew, she reminded herself. She should instead focus on Zane, ensure that Zane learned everything about his amazing father.

December.

The Christmas Eve service was heart-warming as expected. Zane slept the whole time he played the part of the baby in the manger. Mum and Grandma were so proud of him.

As they were leaving, John and Helen invited the ladies to lunch the following day after the Christmas service. Cilla's heart jumped despite knowing she had no reason for anticipation.

'Thank you for the invitation.' Susan shook her head with sincere regret. 'We're expected at Connie's after church tomorrow. It's our first Christmas after so many years, and they've got it in their heads to make the biggest fuss for me, Cilla and the baby.'

Helen smiled. 'That sounds wonderful.' She paused with a tentative glance toward Cilla. 'Drew promised to video-call us.'

Cilla cleared her throat and forced herself to ask about their recently reclusive son. 'How is he going? How's his project?'

'It's going well. At least that's what he told us.' Helen's smile remained warm, but she said no more.

Cilla wondered if Helen could hear her heart thumping in her chest. Wondered if she could tell how desperate she was to hear more.

She couldn't help that she did miss Andrew. While she was avoiding him because of her growing feelings, she had taken for granted that he was always near. And when he left …

'It's been … different not having him around,' she admitted softly.

Helen's gaze on her was steady. 'Yes, I can't remember a time he's been gone this long. We've missed him.'

She felt everyone's eyes on her, and her self-consciousness threatened to engulf her. Did everyone know her thoughts? The evening was suddenly too warm.

'Mum, I think we ought to get Zane home.'

Susan agreed and they all kissed and hugged, wishing one another a lovely Christmas before parting ways.

On Christmas Day, the Robertsons were at church to celebrate Christ's birth with all the other congregants. No further mention of Andrew. At the conclusion of the service, Helen handed her and Susan a boxed gift – a swanky hamper, it turned out – with a Christmas card. The card was a print of Andrew's artwork, and it was signed on behalf of all the Robertson family. Susan placed it on a mantle with all the other cards they had received.

As the new year approached, her heart grew heavier.

'What wrong, Cilla?'

The tone of Susan's voice was of gentle concern. But how could she voice all that was threatening to crush her?

Susan sat beside her on the sofa when she didn't answer. 'It's coming up so quickly, isn't it?'

Cilla nodded, knowing full well what Susan was talking about. Her internal calendar was never going to let her forget. 'I can't believe it's almost a year since …' Her voice broke. She looked down at the baby wrapped in muslin, sleeping peacefully on the sofa beside her.

Susan reached for her, and she melted into her arms.

Chapter 23

January.

The first anniversary of her husband's and son's death came. Susan was dreading its approach. But when she woke up, the heaviness she expected was not there to greet her in the morning. Instead, the sun was shining, and she had the greatest urge to get up and get digging in their garden.

She was out in the front yard before seven o'clock, pulling out weeds and envisaging what flowers she could buy from the nursery. She was desperate to add some colour to their rather empty front yard.

She and Cilla had survived New Year's Eve by going to bed. It was no use staying up and crying the absence of someone to kiss at midnight. Besides, Cilla needed all the sleep she could get when Zane allowed it! And they did survive the days following, slowly leading up to the date that acutely reminded them of their loss.

'Mum, what are you up to?'

To her surprise, Cilla was also up early, looking chirpy albeit still in a black dress. Zane was in her arms.

Susan preceded her next words with a smile and a wink. 'Don't you think it's about time you put away your mourning clothes?'

Her daughter-in-law knew her well enough to understand she wasn't being disdainful. 'Perhaps tomorrow.' She smiled.

That night, Susan pleaded with God to comfort Cilla, as she again heard the sobbing behind her closed door. But the following morning, Cilla was true to her word, coming to the kitchen dressed in grey slacks and a pastel blue blouse. *Not exactly bursting in colour*, thought Susan, but a very welcome change.

Susan grinned. 'Don't you have a beautiful mummy, Zane?' She greeted mum and bub with kisses. 'It's nice to see you in some colours again.'

March.

The colours of Orange were again changing. And with it, Cilla's wardrobe. Susan noticed deep reds and even pink make an appearance with black jeans or skirts every now and then. She supposed she couldn't force the girl to eliminate all her drab mourning blacks straight away. Black was easy, after all. Not to mention slimming. Although, with Cilla's slight frame, she looked like she was back to her pre-pregnancy body already. She had a nice soft blush to her cheeks of late and her countenance grew more peaceful every day.

One afternoon, when Susan came in after another satisfying workout in the garden, she noticed the difference in the décor.

'I've put some of Michael's photos away.' Cilla's voice came from the kitchen. 'Hope you don't mind. I may have overdone it with pictures all over the house.'

Susan went to her with a smile. 'It looks … less cluttered.' She nodded in approval.

There were still the significant ones scattered about, but not so overwhelming. On the wall remained a big framed photo of the four of them at Michael's and Cilla's wedding.

She gave her a pat and stroked Zane's hair as she passed. 'I'm going to prepare dinner after some tea. Would you like a hot chocolate?'

Cilla nodded.

She cleared her throat as she broached another subject. 'Helen called me earlier.' She didn't turn around to face Cilla, but she heard a shuffle from her direction. 'Andrew will be back in a couple of weeks. He's finished his project and his client is very happy. Unveiled it last month at some big do in Perth. He finished a few projects, actually, so I'm told. That's why he's been gone so long! And he's doing a couple of talks over the next few weeks in Sydney, so he's staying there a little while. I think he's also secured a few more projects to last the year. Not that he needs more work or money. But I suppose that's his occupation, and he really does enjoy it.'

'Hhmm…'

Cilla sounded interested enough so Susan went on. 'Helen invited us to help welcome him home. Any time we can spare a moment when he gets back.' She turned and smirked at Cilla. 'Our calendars are so packed so they're willing to work around us, I guess.' She winked.

Cilla could only nod.

Susan sighed and brought the drinks to the table where Cilla sat with Zane. 'I think it's safe to say that the whole Robertson tribe would like to see you and Zane there.'

'They see us on Sundays at church.'

'But we haven't been exactly social.'

'Mum, I told you … you can go to lunch with them.' She gave Susan a weak smile. 'I just get tired so easily still, so I prefer to go home and nap. Perhaps, it's the breastfeeding.'

'Oh, but they would be thrilled to have us spending time with them again.'

Cilla remained silent, her eyes on her sleeping baby. She took a tentative sip of her hot chocolate, keeping her gaze averted from Susan.

The older woman continued with caution in her next words. 'Apparently, Andrew would very much like to see *us* again.'

'Well, he's welcome to visit here,' she answered softly.

'So, you can hide in your room while he visits with me?' Susan shook her head. 'I know for a fact,' Susan went on, sounding too sure of herself, 'that Andrew would like to see *you* and Zane.'

Cilla took a bigger sip of her hot chocolate.

'There were other guys that I thought were interested in you, but they fell away.' She scoffed and shrugged. 'Finding out you were pregnant was one way of sifting the trash from the treasure, in a manner of speaking.'

Cilla almost spat out her mouthful of drink.

She cleared her throat. 'Let me be more precise. I think Andrew's going away and being a hermit for a couple of months hasn't helped in getting over you.'

Cilla's gaze shot to her. 'Getting over me?'

'Well, I think, there are some very obvious things going on, and we should address those before we – or I – do things we may end up regretting.'

Chapter 24

Susan held her stance as Cilla stared at her. 'Before he left, he was so in love with you.' There was no use keeping things from Cilla any longer.

'How would you know that?'

'He told me.'

'He told you?' Cilla's eyes widened, brown orbs searching for an explanation.

Susan shrugged. 'We may have had a conversation.'

Cilla gasped, hot chocolate forgotten. 'Mum, what did you say to him?'

Susan waved her hand. 'It's months ago now. I can't remember exactly what I said. But anyway ...'

Cilla was speechless, her mouth twitching.

'Look, it's obvious – at least, to me – that he is still as smitten as before. I think things will just take time. I mean, he was confused … He came to visit you several times and it wasn't exactly inviting …'

Cilla's face changed, as though something clicked into place. 'I had all of Michael's photos everywhere.' Cilla audibly swallowed.

'Hm.' Susan nodded once. 'While you were nowhere in sight.'

'And then he left after Zane was born.'

'He was falling in love with the baby as well. He had to do something.'

'He left because he was getting attached to Zane?'

'It's kind of making sense, isn't it?'

Cilla scrunched her forehead. 'What is?'

'He left because he was in love with you.'

'He left because he was in love with me?' she repeated softly, as though she could hardly believe it.

Oh dear. Was she truly this naïve?

Susan wanted to laugh at Cilla's expression, but she knew the moment was serious. 'You were still in mourning. You just had a baby. Your residence was a shrine to your dead husband. And you didn't ever come out to see him when he visited. Put it all together, what impression do you think a guy gets?'

Cilla hugged Zane closer. 'I didn't mean to push him away. Just … deal with my own feelings …'

Susan waited for Cilla to say more, to come to some sort of resolution. But Cilla remained quiet, looking stunned. *How had her romance with Michael blossomed?* Did they not experience the highs and lows, the dizzying euphoria and dysphoria of courtship? Perhaps their romance had been more straight-forward.

She patted the young mum's hand. 'Well, what to do, what to do!' She got up and went into her room to pray, something she'd been doing a lot more lately.

April.

God, am I ready for this? Are these feelings right?

Despite the peace Cilla felt about the love that would remain in her heart for Michael, she'd accepted her undeniably growing feelings for Andrew. She *had* missed him, and the buzzing in her stomach told her she was more than a little excited to see him again. Yet, there were niggling thoughts that continued to taunt her.

Am I being selfish and just thinking of me? Would I be doing the right thing for him? Cilla looked down at her baby, sleeping in her arms with such peace.

Her mind warred with the pros and cons of seeing Andrew, and it was pure physical exhaustion that sent her nodding off, half sitting up in bed, as she nursed her baby. It was a dreamless nap, leaving her groggy when she was startled awake by Susan's voice.

'It's time to go, dear. Are you ready?'

Not really.

Susan knocked.

'Come in, Mum.' She handed Zane to her mother-in-law and busied herself with last minute preparations. But there was nothing left to prepare. She checked her make-up in the mirror, taking deep breaths as there was nothing to touch up.

She volunteered to drive so she could focus on something. Her stomach complained of hunger – being a mother had greatly increased her appetite. But nerves counteracted with nausea.

When they arrived, Helen took Zane, and she was left with nothing to worry about but seeing Andrew again. Her eyes passed around the eager faces, and her stomach fluttered when she locked eyes with him.

He greeted Susan warmly and touched Zane's cheek as his mother showed the baby to everyone there. Then Andrew came to her as though no time had passed since they last saw each other. 'Hey, how are you?' He took her in his arms without any ado, and she found herself holding him just as tight. 'You look lovely in that blue dress.'

She blushed, remembering she'd only ever dressed in black prior to his disappearance.

He lingered and she was inclined to break their embrace. 'How are you? I've heard about your latest projects and how busy you've been.' She kept talking and asking questions, afraid for any awkward pause in their conversation. Her stomach growled, and she blushed.

Andrew laughed. 'How about we get on with lunch, and we can chat all you like after.'

She wasn't at all sure she'd like to chat much more, but she was grateful for food and the break from his attention. It wasn't long, though, until she was seated next to him around the big table that the Robertsons had set up. It wasn't half obvious that Susan had a merry band of others who were also just as happy to see Andrew and Cilla in the same room again.

'How do you think that went?' Susan asked that evening when they were home.

Cilla turned to her. 'Well.' She turned back to folding laundry.

Well? That was it?

Susan didn't know how to proceed. She had observed that Cilla and Andrew spoke to each other during the lunch, but nothing much more than casual conversation. What was she expecting? They hadn't seen each other in some time, Andrew had many others to catch up with during the event. *And,* she reminded herself, *it would take time.*

'Give it time.'

Cilla gave a weak laugh. 'Mum, give *what* time?'

'He did give you a big hug when we arrived.'

'Hm …' Cilla kept folding.

'Well, I don't know what's wrong with him.'

Cilla laughed and sighed. 'Nothing's wrong with him.'

'You're right,' Susan agreed eagerly. And she escaped to her room to pray. And make a few calls.

Chapter 25

May.

Wisdom and direction, those were the things Susan had been praying for lately. Not just for her, but for her daughter-in-law as well. Now that it was over a year since they'd moved to Orange, she had found her feet again and she could see that Cilla and Zane were also thriving here. Thriving in most things, but Cilla could do with some help in one other thing.

Still, she asked for wisdom for her future, where she may be of service to the community. She wanted to volunteer somewhere, when her time wasn't taken up with looking after Zane. Or finding a way to assist two birds obviously in love with each other.

Things weren't progressing even though she could feel the attraction between Andrew and Cilla growing stronger. Both were being far too polite and proper for her liking. And still, she wondered about other concerns Cilla may have. Other than trying to honour her grief, of course. She appreciated her daughter's loyalty. But was loyalty also proving too tough a wall to break?

She could no longer hold back one Sunday afternoon. 'Here's the thing: I'm thinking our relationship with the Robertsons bothers you, given your background. But may I just put my two cents in?' She didn't wait for a reply. 'You are *not* in any way related to Andrew. And if you two were to, uh, pursue something, I don't think there would be a problem.'

Cilla looked away, no doubt thinking about the intricacy of their family tree. Couldn't she instead see the wonderful way their lives had woven together?

'Then, there's the age gap between you. But when I look at you two, your age doesn't seem to matter. You have such a maturity about you, and Andrew is still relatively young.' With a cautious glance at Cilla, she added, 'He looks very good for almost forty.'

If she wasn't mistaken, she thought she saw the young woman's cheeks colour a little.

'I don't want to push you into something you don't want. Ever. So, please do stop me. Tell me to shut up and leave you alone. But …'

Cilla looked up at her. 'Oh, Mum, I could never tell you to shut up.'

'But I will stop – and tell everyone else who thinks you two should get together to stop as well. I want you to be happy, please believe me. That's all I want. And if the memory of Michael is all you ever want or need to go on, I am more than happy with that, too.' She paused and touched her arm. 'But I think that … your feelings for Andrew haven't evaporated as you'd wished. Am I wrong?' she added quickly.

Cilla's eyes grew misty. 'Oh, Mum. I do feel something … but I don't want to. It makes me feel so guilty. I want the feelings to go away, but I can't deny how lovely he is, how caring he has been. And … whenever he's around I feel happy, content … and safe. Maybe I'm just thinking about protecting my future and my baby's? Maybe it's just a selfish thought? That I want someone to be there for me and Zane. That's not right. And that's not fair on Andrew.'

'Is that why you don't want to love him?'

Cilla looked at Susan, as though she wanted to deny it. Then she looked away, her eyes glistening.

Susan shook her head and smiled. 'When you're off-guard, I've seen the way you look at him. Your smile is different when it's Drew you're with. It reminds me of how you used to smile when you looked at Michael.' Susan's voice faded as she looked outside.

'I feel like I'm betraying Michael. He's gone only over a year, and here I am, already falling …' She gasped before she could say any more.

Susan was gentle when she finished her sentence. 'Falling in love with someone else.'

'I don't want to,' she whispered. 'I don't want to forget Michael. And I want Zane to know his real father. I don't want to let go of the love we had. I made my vow to him, and I promised to love him.'

Susan nodded. 'Till death do you part.' She spoke the words softly, but she let the words hang between them. 'You loved Michael with all your heart, my dear girl. No one can deny that. But he is gone. And to love again does not mean that you loved Michael any less. Love is a precious thing. But so is life, which you still have. You have both life and love to give –still *so much*... And there is someone out there who loves you and wants to share life with you.'

Receiving neither a response nor rebuke, Susan went on. 'Andrew will never take the place of Michael. And you will always love Michael. But I know that God can heal our hearts and expand our capacity to love some more.'

'How can I allow myself to be attracted to someone else when I still feel so much love for a dead husband? I will look at his son every day and my heart will break – *each* and *every* time, longing for him to be there. Wishing he could feel this surge of love that I feel every time I hold his son in my arms.' She held Zane closer to her, as though he could absorb her love and grief. 'I am bursting. I have so much love for him – and he's not here! I wonder if maybe I'm just channeling all those feelings towards Andrew. Because *he's* here. It could have been any other man.'

'And yet,' Susan responded with gentleness, 'it *isn't* any other man.'

She allowed the silence to linger between them a while, hoping her words were bringing clarity, unraveling her uncertainties.

'Have you missed Brian Munro since he left?' Susan didn't need Cilla's answer.

Cilla absently stroked her son's back, her eyes cast down.

'Darling, nothing has to happen straight away.' Susan stood and placed a hand on her shoulder. 'God makes all things beautiful in its time. I know that you are going to be a great mum, single or not. And I'm here for you. Just as you've been here for me.' She picked up Cilla's empty cup and walked to the sink. 'But, to be sure, there are plenty of others who care for you, too.'

Chapter 26

June.

A sliver of sunlight across Cilla's eyes woke her just moments before she heard soft knocking on her bedroom door.

Susan beamed at her from the doorway. 'Rise and shine, my princess!'

Cilla grinned. 'It's too early in the morning and too cold to be so cheerful.' Temperatures had dipped below zero the last two nights, and it had snowed the previous evening. She shivered and pulled the quilt tighter around her neck.

'I've got a mug of hot chocolate calling desperately for you. But you have to get up to claim it.'

Susan had an obvious delight in her tone that kindled Cilla's curiosity. Like a sloth, she pushed her covers aside as Susan came to help. Once up and steady on her feet, she checked on Zane in his room. Fast asleep. Content he was fine, she followed Susan to the dining room. But her mother-in-law did not let her sit. Instead, she picked up two mugs and led her to the lounge room. With a greater air of mystery, she put the mugs down on the coffee table, put on a beanie on Cilla's head and wrapped a knitted blanket around her shoulders. Then, she picked up the mugs again and gave one to Cilla.

'There's a nice surprise for you.'

As Cilla sipped her hot beverage, she felt the warmth flow all the way to her toes. But not for long!

'Mum, what are you doing?' she yelped as Susan opened the door to the freezing outdoors. 'It's blanketed in snow outside.'

She dismissed Cilla's complaints away. 'Look!'

Cilla shielded her eyes from the glare of the winter wonderland before her. 'It's too cold.' She shivered and began to make her way to one of the recliners.

Susan gently held her back. 'No, no, no, no, no.' She coaxed her toward the front door. 'Look.'

Her eyes still shielded with one hand, and the hot cup warming the other, Cilla ventured to the door's threshold and looked outside. She gasped and started laughing. 'You made me a snowman?'

'Two,' Susan corrected, sounding chuffed. 'A snow-mum and a snow-child! And –' she added with great effect, '*I* didn't make it.'

Cilla flicked her gaze at her mother-in-law. 'You didn't?' Butterflies flittered from her belly to her chest.

Hunger pangs. Or something else?

She dared not linger on the question. She didn't have her boots on, so she admired the refined, little sculpture of the snowman and its shorter companion from the doorway. They stared at her with big button eyes framed by fake lashes. They were both wrapped in bright scarves, one of her own hats on the taller one and a cute beanie on the little one's head. Carrots for noses. And – unlike the usual snowmen with stick arms – these had snow-sculpted arms with gloves on the ends, touching to look like they were holding hands. It was a lovely splash of colour against the backdrop of white and gray.

Susan chuckled beside her and walked to the window to part the curtains and pull up the blinds. 'You can come away from the door now and admire it from here. We'll crank up the heater as well.' Susan fussed over her as she sat, made her comfortable with throws and blankets in the reclining chair and walked away to make them something to eat.

When Susan came back, she had a more serious motherly look on her face. But she didn't say anything as they ate their croissants and fruits.

Cilla kept looking out at the snowmen, their scarves fluttering in the breeze now and then. But in her mind's eye was a lovely gentleman whom she'd grown to appreciate. That much she couldn't deny.

July.

She just couldn't leave well enough alone.

As far as Susan was concerned, Andrew was the man for Cilla. He just wouldn't go any faster than a leisurely pace with the whole courtship business. Cilla was never going to make any moves to say or do anything to quicken the process. Watching those two was a tortuous lesson in patience. Clearly, Andrew had no eyes for any other woman but Cilla. Susan did wonder what happened between him and Maggie. None of her business, of course. They do seem amicable enough, and she was glad of that.

But with Cilla, he was clearly smitten. And Susan couldn't stand the tension fizzing out of both of them when they were together and nothing happening.

After watching another sweet but platonic interaction between them after the church service, she heard herself speak her mind to Judy. 'I wish they'd just tell each other how they really feel.'

Judy snickered. 'Don't we all!'

Susan shook her head contritely. 'Did I say that out loud?'

The ladies giggled softly.

'It's like watching a soap opera.' Helen's voice popped in, amusement in its tone.

Susan blushed as she looked at Helen.

'What?' Helen demanded in good nature. 'You think you're the only one who's been waiting on those two to figure out they're perfect for each other?'

Susan felt it was her duty to, at the very least, defend her daughter-in-law. 'We-ell … She *has* been through a lot in the past eighteen months.'

Helen put a hand on her shoulder. 'You are right, Susie. You know her best.'

Susan nodded.

There was a cheeky sparkle in Helen's eyes. 'And you're in the best position to plant some seeds.'

Susan scoffed lightly. 'And you don't think I've done that?'

Helen tilted her head and grinned, mischief afoot. 'Well, then, if the planting's been done, it's time for action.'

While Susan liked Helen's line of thinking, she was concerned. 'Don't farmers wait a while between planting and harvest?'

With a shake of her head, Helen took her on one arm and Judy on the other. 'Susie, Susie, Susie. If you've had your finger on the pulse – and I believe you have—' she looked sideways at her and winked, 'I believe enough time has lapsed since the planting began.'

'She's been mourning,' Susan defended weakly.

Helen nodded. 'And my dear Drew knows that. Totally respects that. But he could not help falling in love with her, anyway. Don't you think so, too, Judy?'

Judy nodded with enthusiasm. 'Watched it blossom in the café!' Her grin was ear to ear.

'We all fell in love with dear Cilla,' Helen went on. 'And when I saw my son showing her more attention than he does his crazy abstract paintings, I just knew something was meant to happen. I truly felt in my heart she's the one my son's been waiting for.'

Judy's head could fall off with all her nodding. 'Cilla was a godsend in every way.'

Susan sighed. All true. But what was she to do now?

As if reading her mind, Helen squeezed her arm. 'I've been praying to God above for wisdom, patience, clarity and guidance. And I sense that you have been, too.'

Susan nodded.

'When Andrew left to take on projects he initially didn't want do, working so far away, and for so long, it broke our hearts. But we knew why. So, John and I kept praying. Kept watering seeds that we knew were already there. Trusted God. Waited. And we're still waiting.'

Susan looked at Judy, who nodded in affirmation. 'I've been praying, too. I've seen how Andrew is with her. He truly cares for her. I even teased him about it. But he never said anything.'

At this, Susan was surprised. Andrew had told her. Told her specifically that he loved Cilla. Was she the only one privy to this confession?

And, of course, she was the only who knew how Cilla truly felt.

'We-ell …'

She tossed the pros and cons about discussing Cilla's struggle.

No. She had made a promise.

Had she? Again, she was looking for loopholes.

She sighed. 'Okay.' With reluctance, she carefully crafted her response. 'I have been praying, too.' She looked at them with shielded eyes. 'We both think Andrew is wonderful. He … he reminds me of my son.' She lifted her eyes, stopping the mist from forming. 'And Cilla…'

Careful.

'She respects him a lot.' She laughed at her weak choice of words.

The other two ladies looked eager to hear more.

Careful.

She swallowed. 'Look. I think they'd make a great couple. I've also dropped hints and asked what she thought…but…'

Careful.

She shook her head at the two women. 'I really can't say much more.'

Judy and Helen looked at each other.

Oops! She'd said too much.

Helen's smile was triumphant. 'Then we shall wait and pray some more.'

Chapter 27

August.

Zane's first birthday party was tiring, but Cilla's heart was full. Her son was loved and doted on like a prince. And in turn, she felt more and more at home in Orange with her mother-in-law. Sydney seemed like a lifetime ago, and Michael's memory no longer anchored her there. Instead, she carried it with her wherever she went. She would always have him in her heart.

She and Susan gathered wrapping and litter from the floor as Zane played with his new toys.

It was Susan who broke the sweet silence. 'We just need to acknowledge something, even though I know you're a long way from being over the grief. We *both* are still mourning.'

Cilla looked up at her. Even though her heart skipped a beat, it no longer thumped as it used to when Susan began conversations in that manner.

The other woman hesitated, as though she didn't know what to say next. Then she took a deep breath, her mind seemingly made up. 'I know how much you and Michael adored each other.'

Those words threatened to crack another reservoir of tears, but Cilla had improved on managing her emotions.

'I know it hasn't been that long,' Susan went on, her own eyes beginning to mist. 'I'm still broken, too. For both Peter – the love of *my* life – and Michael. I don't wish to pretend I understand how you feel … losing a husband so early, when you both had so much to look forward to together. But I do know what it feels to lose a husband and your best friend.'

'Oh, Mum,' Cilla mumbled, her tears breaking out for her mother-in-law – and what could have been her future with Peter. She felt the same pain, the same loss, and the crazy innate desire to survive despite the agony of separation.

Zane babbled over a soft toy, reminding her of Michael ... and flaming in her the desire to have him there. Yet seeing another man's face besides his fanned the other flame of guilt. And the pang of shame for being disloyal.

Susan wiped the tears from her face with her index fingers and took a deep breath. 'What am I getting at? I've got so much I want to say.' She gave a short laugh. 'Cilla, please forgive me if I just get straight to the point and pour out all the thoughts that have been going through my head. I've harped on the same things before, but I need to confess something else. And also give you some advice. Let me do it, as your mother-in-law. And then you can tell me to go away and never mention it again.'

Cilla smiled despite her tears. 'Go for it.'

'Andrew still loves you.'

Cilla turned away, focusing on Zane. Yes, here we are again. Had the other woman read her mind?

Susan looked at her kindly. 'I'm sorry I'm bringing him up again. But … Well … I'm guilty of playing cupid. I must confess that.'

'What?' Cilla held back a blend of exasperation, anxiety, anticipation and guilt. Her cheeks warmed.

The other woman gave her a rueful expression. 'I am sorry, and I ask for your forgiveness.'

Cilla bit her lip, her brow furrowed. 'Of course.' Then she grinned. 'Just don't do it again, please.'

Susan smiled warmly. 'I hope to *never* do it again. But, here we are, anyway. And I think it's high time we talked about what to do with the other Mr Robertson.' She cast Cilla a weary glance. 'May we?'

Cilla leaned back on the recliner she was sitting on and took a deep breath. As she continued to watch Zane, who she knew adored Andrew, she cast her mind to a more recent memory. She recalled the snowmen – their baby carrots for noses making her smile – and felt the comforting caress of the Holy Spirit. '*To everything there is a season, and a time to every purpose under the heaven…'*

She turned to Susan with a thoughtful but welcoming smile. 'What would you like to discuss?'

Chapter 28

'Connie! How would you like to have brunch at the Garden Café?' Susan explained the situation to her cousin over the phone. 'I got word from a very reliable source that there's an artist roaming around the Botanic Gardens today.'

'Oh, really?' Susan could hear the excitement in Connie's voice.

'Yeah. Doing some special art project for the local council, I heard.'

Connie giggled. 'And I think you have a lovely young mum who needs some sun and time out from her toddler.'

'Too right. Shall I call Frances while you extend the invitation to Mary?'

'Done.'

Susan hung up just as Cilla entered the room with Zane on her hip.

'I'm having lunch with Fran *et al*, come and join us!' Susan extended her arms, and Cilla accepted the offer of relief.

The sun shone bright through their window. She felt she could do with a bit of *somewhere-other-than-the-house*. And lunch with the aunties would be a great distraction from the myriad of questions and scenarios wreaking havoc in her mind. Thoughts that sent her heart soaring one minute and plunging down at terminal velocity the other. Thoughts about Andrew and all the possibilities he brought. She couldn't take the giddiness anymore.

'Where are you going?' Not that it mattered. She was already packing Zane's bag.

'Just at the restaurant in the gardens.'

'Yes, please!' Cilla loved the Botanic Gardens and had been eager to go for a walk since spring arrived. She could leave Zane with the ladies while she took a stroll, refresh her mind, enjoy God's canvas.

Susan grinned. 'Excellent!' She whipped a very light shawl around her shoulders.

'Do you think it might get cold?'

Susan nodded. 'There's a bit of a breeze – bringing something to put over me just in case. And they sometimes crank the air con on in the restaurant.'

Cilla grabbed a thin jumper for herself. It took less than five minutes to drive across to the Botanic Gardens, and the three of them found Frances, Mary and Connie sitting at a big table by the window.

'I was hoping you and Zane would come out to play!' Connie hugged her tight.

Each of the ladies kissed her cheek and commented on how lovely she looked, and how Zane had grown and changed in features since they last saw him! Cilla noticed her mother-in-law had a spark in her eyes as she described his milestones and the joy he has brought to her.

'He is such an amazing little boy,' she bubbled. 'When he looks at you, your heart just melts.'

'Aww,' said the ladies together.

Susan sighed with contentment, her eyes watering. 'Life has a way of serving you the unexpected, doesn't it? I could never have imagined things turning out this way.' She looked past them, out the window. 'When Pete and Mike died, I couldn't get myself out of the shadows. I was depressed, and there didn't seem to be anything to look forward to. I was lost ... I was dead inside. But this girl – this woman! – stood by me all the way and didn't let me drown. And now, look, I have a grandson, too! I know nothing can replace my men. But I've been given a gorgeous little boy to love.' She breathed deeply, like coming up from the depths for air for the first time. 'It's like falling in love again.' She turned to Cilla with a meaningful smile.

Cilla let her mother-in-law's comment slide. Cilla was happy for Susan, that she had found her way back home. Back to Orange. And just may have found her way back home to God.

'It looks beautiful out there,' Cilla sighed, gazing outside the window at the scene bathed with sunlight.

'Why don't you go for a walk?' Susan suggested. 'We'll mind Zane. He's fast asleep, he shouldn't get into too much trouble.' She glanced at the others.

'Are you sure?' Cilla was torn. But the call of the flowers and trees outside was strong. 'I could take Zane, he'll probably just sleep in the stroller.'

'Leave him, and we'll be right here when you get back,' Susan assured her. 'You need some time for yourself as well, you know.'

Frances pulled out her needles and wool. 'I'll be here knitting a while.' She laughed. 'And if they throw us out, we'll be just right outside on one of the benches. Go and breathe some fresh air.'

Cilla looked around at the women, who all looked back at her with encouraging smiles. 'Oh, all right,' she agreed and stood up to go. 'I won't be more than fifteen-twenty minutes. And I've got my phone. Call me if Zane gets too much!'

'Take your time.' Susan waved her away and turned back to the others. The discussion was over.

Cilla was confident that Zane was likely to be knocked out for at least an hour, so she stepped out of the restaurant and ambled over to the arched entrance of the gardens. People were everywhere, likely making the most of the gorgeous day as she was. But unlike the lazily strolling population, she knew exactly where she wanted to go. Past the function centre and the apple and pear orchards, she slowed as she neared the eucalypt woodland overlooking the billabong. Breathing deeply, she assured herself that Zane would be okay with so many doting relatives to pass him around if he woke and cried. She relaxed as she stopped beneath a tall gum. Leaning against the tree, she slowly took in her surroundings. Gone were the bright oranges and reds of autumn; the colours now verdant with lush leaves, with blooms of bright whites, yellows, pinks and purples, promising an even more delightful canvas in the weeks ahead.

Groups of tourists and couples jogging buzzed about. As a dragonfly whizzed past her head, the sunshine and its warmth and a soft breeze lulled her deeper into relaxation. Her heart steadied and she closed her eyes to soak in the atmosphere. When she'd had enough of a rest, she decided to head back and reclaim motherhood responsibilities for her son. Pushing off from the tree, she cast one last glance at the billabong and allowed her eyes to roam around once more.

As she turned to begin her leisurely walk back, she gasped. Her heart jumped to her throat and she choked back a nervous laugh, as there, only a few metres from her, Andrew was heading in her direction.

Chapter 29

There was no use pretending she hadn't seen him. 'Well, hi!' She smiled brightly as Andrew got closer. 'Fancy meeting you here!'

He grinned back, his expression calm and inviting. 'You come here often?'

She laughed at that, and he looked relieved. 'No,' she replied. 'But, I should.' Her face warmed and she looked away, embarrassment bubbling to her cheeks. 'I mean, it's beautiful here, and I should walk more often.' She turned back to him. 'And you? Is this a regular haunt?'

He nodded and lifted his sketch book a little. 'When I want to relax and just sketch, I come here or visit one of the other parks. But lately I've been coming for a project.'

Cilla stared at him, unable to come up with an intelligent response. Why was it now so awkward to be here with this man? They had been good friends at one point, had easy conversations. *It's because you're in love with him,* her mind taunted her. Having him here, just the two of them, was shooting her emotions out of the atmosphere. She'd heard often enough, from so many sources, that he loved her. But not directly from him.

How were they to act around each other now; now that everybody else had played cupid, but the two of them hadn't been open to each other?

Andrew cleared his throat. 'Uhm … where's your little bodyguard?'

At the reminder of him, she started walking, forcing to keep her steps unhurried. 'He's, uh, actually in the restaurant.'

Andrew turned and strode with her, matching her pace. 'Did he order the steak?' He asked lightly.

Cilla giggled. 'It may be some time yet before he makes the move from mashed peas and pumpkin.'

'So, he's on a date and you're chaperoning?'

Cilla giggled again. His lightheartedness made her feel more at ease.

He touched her arm lightly, and she stopped. She turned to face him, searched his eyes, wondering what he was thinking, finding herself … expectant.

Her surroundings blurred, and only he came into focus. His eyes were on her, roaming and taking in every detail of her face. He took a deep breath and she held hers.

'I …' He shook his head and dumped his book and pencils on the ground. He took both her hands and looked into her eyes again. 'Cilla, I am in love with you.'

Her breath came out strangled. Never had she allowed herself to dream things would happen this way. Nor anything like this to happen at all.

Andrew continued. 'I have been for a while now. I don't know when it started. But, I'm sure, from the moment I first saw you, I felt something for you. I'm almost ashamed to say, I felt something when I saw you crying at Michael's funeral.'

Cilla's chin twitched. Her sinus ached and her eyes stung, warning that tears were about to make an appearance. Was she supposed to say something? Because no words were forthcoming.

'I wanted to hold you then. I wanted to comfort you and protect you.'

Cilla blinked and a pool formed in the corner of her eyes. But she held his gaze, desperate for his words. She managed to give his hand a faint squeeze. *Go on. It's okay.*

'I'm not a romantic. At least, I didn't think so. I'd almost given up on finding somebody to love. But then ... you came along. You literally came in a dying car and I happened to be the one to help you on the road. And I don't think that was a coincidence.'

She laughed softly, remembering her embarrassment, and nodded for him to continue.

'And then you walk into my café, on a day I'm there, and ask for a job. I did not have anything to do with that at all. You won Judy over with your personality and attitude. And wouldn't you know it, you walk into my church one Sunday, and make my whole family fall in love with you.'

'I'm sorry, I didn't mean to,' she whispered.

'I didn't want to,' he admitted. 'It almost felt like we were related!'

She nodded as they both laughed.

'And Maggie?' Cilla asked.

Andrew sighed, looked at their hands, then looked into her eyes again. 'I wished – at the time – that I felt something for her. But it just never happened. I tried, and I questioned myself. But, then … when you came into the picture, my feelings for her became clearer. There was nothing but respect and admiration. But, you –'

He shook his head, touched her cheek with his fingertips.

'You make me see so many possibilities,' he told her. 'You make me see a future and a hope. And you helped me see the world in a whole new splash of colour.'

'Says the artist,' she whispered, lifting a hand to place over his. Then she sobered. It was all good and well – with him confessing his love, unhindered and free. But what about her? Was she doing the right thing – letting her feelings run away like this? What about Michael, and the way she had loved him? And if she loved again… What guarantee did she have that she would not lose again?

Andrew's eyes looked deeply into hers. 'What is it, Cilla?' His brow furrowed.

Her mouth twitched. 'I am a little scared,' she admitted.

'What are you scared of?' he asked, pulling her a little closer.

A tear slid down her cheek and he stopped it with his thumb.

'Of the pain of loving and losing.' She sighed heavily. 'Of what people will think of me, with someone else … so soon. … And wondering if you're not just feeling sorry for me.' She looked up at him, her eyes beseeching. *Please tell me I'm wrong. Please tell me everything will be okay.*

Andrew smiled, taking his time to answer, his eyes firmly on hers. 'I can't promise you every tomorrow. But I promise to love you as best as I can and for as long as I live.' His thumb caressed her cheek. 'As for what people will think – what does it matter? The ones who love you and truly know you – they know your heart. More importantly, the Lord knows every question and heartache you've wrestled with. He knows how loyal and steadfast you've been. Cilla, He knows your heart.'

He paused, his eyes making sure she was taking it all in. 'And how could I pity you? A woman of strength, of faith, love … and so self-less. Someone so determined and capable, caring and kind! You're a dream… You're *my* dream.'

The dam walls broke and she cried. 'I didn't want to fall for you, either,' she said. 'I loved Michael so much.'

Both his hands now cupped her face. 'I know you did. And you still do. It's okay.' He placed his forehead on hers. 'I will give you all the time you need to work things out. I'm not here to make you think I could ever replace Michael. I respect his place in your heart. I just wanted you to know how I've been feeling for you. How I've loved you for a while now. And I still do.'

Her hands gripped his shirt as she wept openly. 'I will always love Michael,' she said slowly, 'but I have a confession to make, Andrew …'

He smiled at her, encouraging her to go on.

'Now, I'm in love with you,' she whispered.

His own tears fell even as he started to laugh. He pulled her to him and held her. Tight. As though he didn't want to let her go.

Finally, he pulled away, brushed her wind-blown hair behind her ears and, looked deep into her eyes. Cilla's heart hammered. Could he see her own desire for him?

She didn't have long to contemplate it as he leaned close. He kissed her lips, soft and warm. And her arms lifted to his shoulders, wrapped around his neck, and brushed away any remaining distance between them.

Epilogue

November.

The jacarandas on their street were in full bloom. Susan appreciated its purple hue even more when she saw Cilla walk out of her bedroom in a sleeveless maxi dress in that very colour.

Susan bounced her rosy-cheeked grandson on her lap. 'Doesn't mummy look as pretty as a flower!'

Cilla smiled shyly.

'Mum-mah!' Zane looked up, pointed to her, then continued pointing to pictures on the book that he and grandma were reading.

Susan watched covertly as Cilla did some last-minute preparations for her first date with

Andrew. She was positively blooming. *Like the flowers.* Susan chuckled. The smile on Cilla's face lately was sign enough that the young mother had reached a turning point in her life. And Susan was more than glad for her.

The knock on the door startled Cilla.

'I'll get it,' Susan told her, hoisting Zane on her hip. 'You go and finish off whatever you're doing.'

Cilla laughed. 'I'm just preparing Zane's food and milk so it'll be easy for you.'

Susan waved her hand in dismissal. 'I know where everything is.' She turned and opened the door. 'Well, hello, Great-Aunts Frances, Mary and Connie! And hello, Grandma Helen.' She winked.

'Shh!' Helen hissed with a soft giggle. 'We don't want to scare the lovebirds.'

Susan ushered them in.

'Hi, everyone!' Cilla greeted them each with a kiss, then allowed them to settle around the lounge room as they prepared for their craft session and late morning tea.

Helen gave her a tight hug. 'Andrew said he'll be here soon.' She let go. 'I hear you've got a big day ahead of you.'

Cilla could not hide her happy smile. 'Really? I thought we were just having lunch.'

Helen shrugged mildly. 'Okay, then.' She plopped on the sofa and pulled out a cloth with embroidered flowers half done. 'I'm sure you'll enjoy.'

The other aunts tittered. 'Yes, don't spoil it for her, dear!'

Cilla shook her head at them, grinning broadly. She turned and went back to the kitchen.

Zane was passed around for a few minutes, allowing the other ladies to cuddle and spoil him. When it was Helen's turn, she put down her embroidery and held the baby in front of her. She whispered a few things to him, none of which Susan heard. Then Helen drew him near and embraced him so tight, Susan's heart melted for her. Helen looked up and they exchanged a knowing glance.

When Andrew arrived a few minutes later, Zane crawled to the door to greet him. Pulling himself up to a standing position with the help of the screen door, he waited excitedly as Grandma sauntered to the door. He pointed to the man on the other side of the door and made a bubbling noise as drool oozed from his lips.

'Who's mummy's cute little man?' Andrew greeted him.

He banged on the door, as though to tell Grandma to hurry up.

When the door opened, Zane squealed in delight, and held up his arms so that Andrew would pick him up. As his visitor did so, Cilla appeared. Andrew looked at her and his breath caught audibly.

Susan's insides warmed, and she glanced at Helen, who winked at her. They watched as Andrew took a few strides to reach his beloved and kiss her gently on the forehead, Zane still in his arms.

A little timid and shy, they still were. But Susan was confident that as the seasons changed, their love would only grow.

Zane was in her arms as they watched Andrew drive Cilla away for their long-awaited first official date. She was at the door, while the other women were peeking through the blinds, all giggly like teenagers watching their first high school crush.

Finally, she closed the door and put Zane on the floor as they got on with tea, craft and their usual chatter.

When she sat back and simply watched her companions, Frances squinted at her over her glasses. 'Well, what? What are you grinning about?'

Susan shook her head with a soft smile, gratitude making her vision blur. 'My God has restored my joy,' she began. 'He has done more than I could ever hope or imagine.'

Acknowledgements

I am nothing without my Jesus, whose glory I pursue in what I do.

Anna W, June S, Gill E, Lisa Y, Fiona N - who encouraged me to continue with this story ... and suggested I go a little easier on poor Dr Munro.

My Sisterhood of Jura House ladies - that weekend retreat changed my writing life. I'm grateful for your love and support, and the laughter and strawberries.

Omega Writers and its Sydney Chapter - what would I have done without you?

Penny - thank you for the guidance you provided and helping me stay focused during the writing of this manuscript.

Elizabeth - for the opportunities you have given me to share my stories and to touch readers' hearts. Your vision, creativity and perseverance inspires me.

Last, and certainly not least, my family. My parents, in-laws and extended family who have supported me. My children, who don't quite understand what I write but never question why, and who are big fans anyway. My husband, my real-life hero.

D.O.L.L.

Daughters of Love & Light is a ministry hub for women and an independent publisher of Christian women's literature.

We believe in Christ-centred community, creativity, and calling.

Join the community
www.daughtersofloveandlight.com